FUNNY STORIES FOR
SIX YEAR OLDS

Helen Paiba is known as one of the most committed, knowledgeable and acclaimed children's booksellers in Britain. For more than twenty years she owned and ran the Children's Bookshop in Muswell Hill, London, which under her guidance gained a superb reputation for its range of children's books and for the advice available to its customers.

Helen was involved with the Booksellers Association for many years and served on both its Children's Bookselling Group and the Trade Practices Committee. In 1995 she was given honorary life membership of the Booksellers Association of Great Britain and Ireland in recognition of her outstanding services to the association and to the book trade. In the same year the Children's Book Circle (sponsored by Books for Children) honoured her with the Eleanor Farjeon Award, given for distinguished service to the world of children's books.

She retired in 1995 and now lives in London.

Funny

STORIES

for Six Year Olds

COMPILED BY HELEN PAIBA

ILLUSTRATED BY KATE SHEPPARD

MACMILLAN
CHILDREN'S BOOKS

First published 1999 by Macmillan Children's Books
a division of Macmillan Publishers Limited
20 New Wharf Road, London N1 9RR
Basingstoke and Oxford
Associated companies throughout the world
www.panmacmillan.com

ISBN 978-0-330-36857-5

35 37 39 40 38 36

A CIP catalogue record for this book is available from
the British Library.

Typeset by SX Composing DTP, Rayleigh, Essex
Printed and bound by CPI Group (UK) Ltd, Croydon, CR0 4YY

Contents

How to Get Rich

David Henry Wilson

"How do you make money?" asked Jeremy James one morning at breakfast.

"No idea," said Daddy. "But if you ever find out, let me know."

"You have to work for it," said Mummy. "You work, and then people pay you."

"What sort of work?" asked Jeremy James.

"All sorts," said Mummy. "Different people do different work."

"Well, what sort of work could I

1

do to get some money?" asked Jeremy James.

"What do *you* need money for?" asked Mummy.

"Spending," said Jeremy James.

"Spending on what?" asked Mummy.

Why was it that grown-ups never answered questions? You could ask them about anything, but they would never tell you what you wanted to know. Only yesterday he'd asked Mummy why the man they'd just walked past had one leg instead of two, and Mummy had said "Sh!" to him as if he'd said something rude. "I only want to know what's happened to his other leg," Jeremy James had said, but Mummy had shushed him again with a threatening look. And the

day before that, when he'd watched
Mummy bathing the twins and
had asked why Jennifer hadn't got
something he and Christopher *had*
got, all he received was a
"Hmmmph!" instead of an answer.
You never get answers from grown-
ups. Just "sh", "hmmph", or
questions about why you were
asking questions.

"Toys," said Jeremy James. "So
that I can buy more toys." He
would have said sweets, but he
knew what Mummy would say
about more sweets.

"Haven't you got enough toys?"
asked Mummy.

"Well I haven't got a tricycle
with a saddlebag," said Jeremy
James. "So how can I get money
for a tricycle with a saddlebag?"

"I haven't got a tricycle with a saddlebag either," said Daddy. "It seems to be a common weakness in the family."

Daddy tended not to say "sh" or "hmmmph" or ask questions; he just said things that had nothing to do with what you were asking.

"Well, what work can I do?" asked Jeremy James, who could be very determined when there was something to be determined about.

"Let's have a look in the paper," said Daddy. "See if we can find something suitable."

And Daddy spread the paper out at the page where it said "Jobs Vacant".

"Now then," he said. "How about 'long-distance lorry-driver'? No, not after your efforts at short-distance car-driving. 'Cook required part-time at nursing home.' What's your cooking like, Jeremy James?"

"I'm good at strawberries and ice cream," said Jeremy James.

"But you'd never leave any for the patients," said Daddy.

"That's true," said Jeremy James. "But I'd like that sort of work."

"I expect you would," said Daddy. "It's the kind of job you can grow fat on. How about being a coalman?"

"Too dirty," said Jeremy James.

"A street cleaner, then?" said Daddy.

"I don't like cleaning," said Jeremy James.

"Ah," said Daddy. "So it's got to be something that won't make you dirty and won't make you clean."

"And they must pay me lots of money," said Jeremy James.

"Nothing like that here, I'm afraid," said Daddy, closing the paper. "Fairy godmothers don't advertise in our papers."

Mummy and Daddy smiled at each other, but Jeremy James didn't think it was funny. Sweets (and toys and tricycles with saddlebags) cost money, and if you wanted money you had to work, and if you couldn't work, you couldn't have money, and without money you couldn't have sweets (or toys or tricycles with saddlebags). And that wasn't at all funny. Jeremy James frowned. And behind his frown there began to stir a vague memory from the distant past. It had been at least two days ago. He had gone round the corner with Mummy to the greengrocer's shop, and in the greengrocer's window had been a large notice which Mummy had helped him to read. "Bright Lad Wanted" – that's what the notice had said. Jeremy James thought hard for a moment.

"Mummy," said Jeremy James. "Am I bright?"

"As bright as a button," said Mummy.

Jeremy James thought hard for another moment.

"Daddy," said Jeremy James. "How much do bright lads get paid?"

"Depends what they're doing," said Daddy.

7

"Sort of . . . well . . . green-grocing?" said Jeremy James.

"No idea," said Daddy. "I expect they get the union rates for bright greengrocing lads."

"What's union rates?" asked Jeremy James.

"That's what you'll get paid when you get the job," said Daddy.

Jeremy James did some more hard thinking. The problem was not what to do, but how to get permission to do it. He looked at Mummy, and he looked at Daddy, and he looked at the table, and he took a deep breath and said: "Can I just go round the corner to the . . . um . . . sweetshop?"

To his surprise, Mummy gave him permission without asking a

single question.

"Good luck!" said Daddy, as Jeremy James left the house.

"But don't go into the road," said Mummy, "and come straight home afterwards."

Jeremy James walked proudly and brightly up the street and round the corner to the green-grocer's shop. The notice was still in the window. Jeremy James puffed out his chest, and marched in.

"And what can we do for you?" asked a thin man in a brown coat, with a face like a wizened apple.

"I'm a bright lad," said Jeremy James.

"Aha!" said the wizened apple. "I can see that. But what can I do for you?"

"Well, I've come for the job," said Jeremy James. "So that I can get enough money for a tricycle with a saddlebag. And you should pay me onion rates."

"Onion rates, eh?" said the man in the brown coat. "What's your name, then, sonny?"

"Jeremy James," said Jeremy James.

"That's a smart-sounding name all right," said the man in the brown coat. "But to tell you the truth, Jeremy James, we were really looking for someone a little older and a little bigger."

"I'll be getting bigger," said Jeremy James. "I've grown quite a lot since last week."

"Oh you'll be growing fast, I'm sure," said the man. "You'll be growing at onion rates, won't you? But you see, we need someone to carry big loads of fruit and vegetables around. And he'd have to be able to carry them on a bicycle to the houses around here."

"Well I could put them in my saddlebag," said Jeremy James. "When I've got a saddlebag."

"And when you've got a tricycle," said the man.

"Yes," said Jeremy James.

"No, I don't think that would work," said the man. "Because there's an awful lot to carry."

"I'll get a *big* saddlebag," said Jeremy James.

"In any case," said the man, "you couldn't do the job till you had your tricycle. And you can't have your tricycle till you've done the job. It's what's called a vicious circle. Or cycle."

Jeremy James's head dropped down on his chest like a cabbage too heavy for its stalk.

"I'll tell you what," said the man. "You try and grow nice and quickly, and when you're as tall as my shoulder, come back and I'll give you the job."

"I'll never be as tall as your shoulder," said Jeremy James.

"If you eat plenty of fresh fruit and vegetables," said the man, "you'll be up past my shoulder in no time. And I'll start you off myself, how's that? Come here, Jeremy James. Now take this paper bag."

Jeremy James took the large

paper bag that the man held out to him.

"Now you go round my shop," said the man, "and fill that paper bag with anything you like."

"Anything?" said Jeremy James.

"Anything," said the man.

Jeremy James looked round the shop. Apples, oranges, pears, bananas . . . potatoes, tomatoes, beans, carrots . . .

"You haven't got any chocolate, have you?" asked Jeremy James.

"Afraid not," said the man.

"Or any tins of mandarin oranges?" asked Jeremy James.

"No tins here," said the man. "Everything fresh as God made it."

Jeremy James filled his bag until its sides were splitting and he

needed both hands and both arms to hold it all together.

"Off you go, then, Jeremy James," said the man, "and I'll see you when you're up to my shoulder."

"All right," said Jeremy James. "I'll be back next week. Thank you very much for the bagful."

When Mummy and Daddy saw the bag of fruit, their eyes opened as wide as apples.

"Where did that come from?" asked Mummy.

"I went for a job at the greengrocer's," said Jeremy James.

"Did you get it?" asked Daddy.

"Well, not exactly," said Jeremy James. "He said I should come back next week when I'm as tall as his shoulder."

"Ah," said Daddy, "and he gave you all this to help you grow."

"Yes," said Jeremy James. "I'll be growing at onion rates."

"Well, that is a lovely lot of fruit," said Mummy, emptying the bag onto the table. "Worth a small fortune."

An idea came into Jeremy James's mind, and lit up his eyes from inside.

15

"Well, it is mine," he said, "but you can have it for nothing if you give me some money for it."

Mummy looked at Daddy, and Daddy looked at Mummy.

"Fair enough," said Daddy. "If you want free fruit, you must pay for it."

"How much are you asking?" said Mummy.

"It's worth a small fortune," said Jeremy James. "But I'd like enough to buy a tricycle with a saddlebag."

"Oh," said Mummy, "now that would be a large fortune."

"All right," said Jeremy James. "Enough for a box of liquorice allsorts."

And to Jeremy James's surprise and delight, Mummy agreed. Ten

minutes later Jeremy James was
hurrying back up the road and
round the corner to the sweetshop,
and on his face was a smile as wide
as a banana. It was the smile of a
man who had done a good day's
work.

King Keith and the Nasty Case of Dragonitus

Kaye Umansky

King Keith had a right royal cold. He sneezed and wheezed. His throat hurt. He lay in his bed shouting for this and that. When they brought him this, he wanted that. When they brought him that, he wanted something altogether different. He moaned and groaned and bossed and bullied until everyone was worn out. Queen

18

Freda finally got so tired of him that she sent for the Royal Doctor.

"Your Majesty! It's me, Doctor Coldfingers. Can I come in?" called the doctor, knocking on the door.

"*No!*" snapped King Keith. "Go away. I don't want a doctor. Tell the cook to bring me chocolate ice cream. Atchoo!"

"Rubbish," said Doctor Coldfingers, going in anyway. "The last thing you need is chocolate ice cream. I know because I'm a doctor."

"Oh really?"

King Keith glared at Doctor Coldfingers over his hot-water bottle. "So what *do* I need, Coldfingers? In your opinion?"

"Medicine," said Doctor

Coldfingers firmly, producing a large bottle of something green and nasty-looking from behind his back.

"Oh no I don't," said King Keith.

"Oh yes you do. Open up."

"No," said King Keith and dived under the pillows.

"Come out, Your Majesty, and drink your medicine like a brave king," coaxed Doctor Coldfingers.

"Go away," said King Keith.

Just then, Queen Freda came in. Her nose was very red and sore-looking.

"Good morning, doctor. Good morning, dearest," said Queen Freda. "Look, I've picked you a bunch of tulips. They're the ones you planted yourself in the town square. How is your cold?"

"Atchoo! Terrible. Did you send for him?" growled King Keith, pointing at Doctor Coldfingers.

"I most certainly did."

"Why? I don't want him. I don't like doctors."

"But dearest, you must get rid of your cold. You're giving it to everyone in the palace. It's very selfish of you. Atchoo! Drink the medicine, there's a dear."

"No," said King Keith. "Never. I hate medicine. It tastes nasty."

"But you haven't even tried it. Look, I'll take a spoonful."

Queen Freda opened her mouth. Doctor Coldfingers unscrewed the bottle and tipped it up. The green nasty stuff oozed into the spoon with a glopping noise, and Queen Freda swallowed it. She made a little face, but that was all.

"There. That wasn't so bad. Now you."

"Shan't," said King Keith. And closed his lips tight together.

Just then, Prince Percy came into the room, blowing his nose loudly.

"Hello, Dad," said Prince Percy. "How are you feeling?"

"He won't take his medicine," sighed Queen Freda.

"He thinks it tastes nasty," said Doctor Coldfingers.

"I'll try it," said Prince Percy. "I think I've caught his cold." And he took a spoonful.

"Not bad," he said. "Now you, Dad."

"No," sulked King Keith. "I don't like the colour. I want chocolate ice cream."

At that moment, there was the sound of sniffing, and Princess Paula came in.

"Why are you shouting, Daddy?" complained Princess Paula. "My ears are hurting. I'm sure I've got a cold coming."

"Your father won't take his medicine," said Doctor Coldfingers.

"He thinks it will taste nasty," sighed Queen Freda.

"He doesn't like the colour," said Prince Percy.

"Well!" said Princess Paula. "You great big baby! Look, I'll try some." And she did. "Now you."

"No. It's too thick," said King Keith stubbornly.

"Whad's too thig?" said a voice,

and the Lord Chamberlain came into the room. He was talking funny because he too had a very bad cold.

"The King's medicine," said Queen Freda.

"He says it tastes nasty," explained Prince Percy.

"And he doesn't like the colour," added Princess Paula.

"In thad case, he wode mind if I hab sub," said the Lord Chamberlain. "Mmm. Nod too bad. Try it, Your Bajesty."

"No," said King Keith. "I don't like the shape of the bottle. I'm fussy about things like that."

"Isn't he selfish?" sighed Queen Freda. "We've all got colds because of him."

Everyone agreed that King Keith

was very selfish.

Just then, the door flew open, and the Royal Messenger came panting in. Now, the Royal Messenger didn't have a cold. He had something worse! In fact, *he was covered from head to foot in green spots!* Everyone gasped. He wasn't usually like that.

"Your Majesty! Bad news!"

panted the Royal Messenger. "There's a Dragon in the town square!"

"A *Dragon*?" gasped everyone.

"Yes. And what's more, it's got Dragonitus. Everyone's catching it. The whole town's coming out in green spots. And I can tell you, they itch something rotten!"

"Tell it to go away," ordered King Keith firmly.

"It won't, sir. It says it feels too ill to move. It's digging a hole to lie down in. All the tulips you planted are getting ruined. Request permission to scratch, sir."

"Permission denied," said King Keith meanly.

"Go and do it outside, you poor man," said Queen Freda kindly, and the Royal Messenger fled.

"Dragonitus," muttered Doctor Coldfingers. "It sounds serious. I wonder if there's a cure? I think I'll go and see the Medicine Maker."

"We'll all come with you," said Queen Freda. "this is a National Emergency. Come along, Keith."

"Not me," said King Keith. "I'm much too ill. Ask the cook to hurry up with my ice cream, will you?"

And he snuggled down beneath the blankets.

The Medicine Maker lived in a very odd house on the other side of town. It was made of thick brown glass, and shaped like a huge bottle. There were no windows, but it did have a white round door. On it were written the words:

LUDOVIC LINCTUS
MEDICINE MAKER
KNOCK THREE TIMES AFTER MEALS

As Queen Freda, Percy, Paula, Doctor Coldfingers and the Lord Chamberlain approached, they could see clouds of bright blue smoke puffing from the bottle neck.

Percy and Paula nudged each other excitedly. They had always wanted to see inside the Medicine Maker's house.

Doctor Coldfingers knocked three times.

"Can't you read?" shouted a cross voice from inside. "It says *after* meals. I haven't had breakfast yet."

"It's a National Emergency, Mr Linctus!" called Doctor Coldfingers. "Open up. I've got the Queen and Prince Percy and Princess Paula and the Lord Chamberlain with me!"

After a lot of mumbling, the door finally opened and Ludovic Linctus peered out. He was very old, with a long beard stained all

the colours of the rainbow. His robe was covered with messy splash marks, and his hands were bright green.

"I can't get the dye off," he explained. "It splashed all over me yesterday when I was making up the medicine for King Keith. Did it help, by the way?"

"The King won't take it, I'm afraid. He's a terrible baby about taking medicine. But we did, and our colds are much better," said Queen Freda.

"Did you drop the bottle or something?" asked Ludovic Linctus.

"No. Why?"

"Because you're all covered in green spots."

The Queen, the doctor, the Lord

Chamberlain, Percy and Paula looked at each other. Sure enough, they were.

"Oh, dear," said Queen Freda. "Dragonitus. We've caught it already. Can we come in?"

"Yes, of course, of course. You'll have to excuse the mess."

They found themselves in a huge round room. The glass walls were lined with shelves holding hundreds of strange potions in bottles of all shapes and sizes. There were tubs of tablets and pots of powders. There were packets of pills and heaps of herbs.

Tables were piled high with old books, oddly shaped glass instruments and half-eaten sandwiches. In the middle of the floor a large pot of bright blue liquid hissed and bubbled over a fire. Curly blue smoke rose into the bottle-neck chimney high above their heads.

"A National Emergency, you say?" said Ludovic Linctus, giving the pot a little stir.

"Yes. You see, Mr Linctus, there's a sick Dragon in the town square. It's got Dragonitus. Everyone's catching it, and coming out in green spots," explained Doctor Coldfingers. "We're hoping you might know of a cure."

"Dragonitus, eh? Hmm. Just a moment."

The Medicine Maker hobbled over to a tottering pile of ancient books. He picked them up one by

one, peered at the faded titles and
threw them carelessly over his
shoulder any old how. The Queen,
the doctor and the Lord
Chamberlain had to keep ducking
as tatty old volumes flew past their
ears. Percy and Paula looked at
each other and giggled.

"Ah ha!" shouted Ludovic
Linctus, finally finding the ones he
wanted. "Here we are. *Rare Rashes
in Reptiles*. Should be in here.
Now, let me see. Damp patches –
Dandruff – Distemper – Ah! Got it!
Dragonitus."

"Is it serious?" asked Queen
Freda anxiously, peering over
Ludovic Linctus's shoulder.

"Serious? Oh yes, definitely. Very
nasty indeed. It's easier to cure at
the green spot stage, of course. It's

when the hiccups start it gets more difficult. When the hair starts dropping out and the fingernails turn orange, its practically impossible—"

"But there is a cure?" broke in the Lord Chamberlain, turning pale beneath his spots. "You did say there was a cure?"

"Oh yes. Special medicine. It'll take me some time to make it up, though."

"Can we help?" asked Percy and Paula together.

"If you like. But you need strong stomachs. I warn you, Dragonitus Cure has got some very nasty things in it. Dried moths for a start. And fresh beetle juice. Then there's fish bones and a teaspoon of frog spawn. And a pickled mouse nose. Mustn't forget that."

"I think I'll go back to the palace," said Queen Freda hastily. "I'm going to run a nice warm bath, and see if it will stop this horrid itching."

"Me too," said Doctor Coldfingers. "Could you scratch my back, please, Lord Chamberlain? Just between the shoulder blades."

"We want to stay and help. Oh, please! Can we?" begged Percy and Paula.

"Very well. If you don't get in the way," said Queen Freda. "A pickled mouse nose. Uggh!"

"Right," said Ludovic Linctus as soon as they had gone. "Having two helpers should speed things up a bit. I'm going to write out a list of the things I need, and you're going to find them. Ready?"

"Rather," said Percy and Paula. And they hopped from foot to foot and scratched excitedly while Ludovic Linctus wrote out a list of ingredients.

Meanwhile, King Keith lay in bed feeling very irritable. He had spent the last hour shouting and ringing his bell, but nobody had come. He was bored and hungry. Worst of all, he was beginning to itch all over. Idly, he picked up the hand mirror next to his bed and peered at himself.

Oh no! Big green spots, all over him!

"That's it!" shouted King Keith, throwing back the bedclothes and reaching for his Royal robe. "*That is it!* How dare this Dragon come to my town and get all the attention and pass on its beastly illness to me, the King! If nobody else will get rid of it, I'll just have to do it myself."

And up he got, and out he went.

The town was deserted. Everyone was at home, peering in mirrors, rubbing on cream and scratching, scratching, scratching.

As King Keith rounded a corner, a green spotted dog caught sight of itself in a shop window, gave a terrified howl and ran away with its tail between its legs, almost tripping him up.

A green spotted horse came racing down the road, cart rattling behind. It was making for the

river, where it could roll in the
cool mud. There was no sign of its
owner.

Three green spotted pigeons
waddled around in the road,
pecking crossly at their feathers.
They were being watched by a
green spotted stray cat, who was
busily licking its itchy tail with a
green spotted tongue.

"It's a disgrace!" growled King
Keith to the cat. "Just you wait till
I meet that Dragon. I'll have a few
words to say, I can tell you!"

Soon, he reached the town
square – or what was left of it. It
was really more a big hole than a
square. Trees were toppled, all the
grass was uprooted and King
Keith's prize tulips were lying
around all over the place. Huge

piles of earth surrounded the hole, and the place looked like a building site.

King Keith marched up to the edge of the hole and looked down.

A very large, green, spotty, sad face looked back up at him.

"Sorry about this," said the Dragon.

"So you should be," snapped King Keith.

"I don't usually go round digging holes in squares," explained the Dragon. "It's my illness. I feel terrible. You're my first visitor. I'm so glad you've come, because I've been badly neglected. Have you brought me some grapes?"

The Dragon really didn't look at all well. Nobody had come to see how it was, because they were all

in their homes peering in mirrors and scratching at their green spots.

"Grapes? Certainly not. I've come to order you out of my square," shouted King Keith. "What is all this mess? How dare you!"

"Please don't shout. I have this splitting headache," said the Dragon. "Nobody cares that I feel awful. Oh, my poor tummy. Oh, my aching limbs. Oh, my itchy spots."

"*You* feel awful? What about me?" shouted King Keith. "I'll have you know I've had a very bad cold for days. And now I've caught Dragonitus. You've got me out of bed, you have. Don't you know who I am?"

41

"No," said the Dragon. "But whoever you are, I don't like you much."

"Well, I'm the King, and I give the orders around here," snapped King Keith haughtily. "I'm going to count to three, and I want you out of my square. Look what you've done to it! What's that hole for anyway? Atchoo!"

"You can count to five thousand if you like," said the Dragon. "It won't make a jot of difference. I'm not going anywhere. I'm too weak to move. The hole is for me to crawl into. We Dragons always crawl into holes when we're not well. I'll try not to be any trouble. All you have to do is fill it in again. When I'm gone." And a big tear rolled down its scaly cheek.

Just then, there was the sound of running footsteps, and Prince Percy and Princess Paula came racing up. Percy was carrying a huge bottle, and Paula held a gigantic spoon. Hobbling behind them came Ludovic Linctus.

"Oh good," said the Dragon. "More visitors. I hope they'll be more sympathetic than you are."

"Dad! Good news! Guess what's in this bottle!"

"Lemonade," said the Dragon. "For my poor sore throat."

"Wrong," said Prince Percy. "It's Dragonitus Cure."

"We helped make it," added Paula. "Daddy, this is Ludovic Linctus, the Medicine Maker. Oh, poor Dragon. You do look awful."

"I know," said the Dragon. "Tell *him* that," it added, with a bitter glance at King Keith.

"I suppose you're the one who made that revolting cold medicine," said King Keith to Ludovic Linctus. "I refused to drink it."

"Well, that's a pity, Your Majesty. My medicines might taste nasty, but they usually do the trick."

"Let's hope this one works," snapped King Keith, snatching the bottle. "Right. Come along, Dragon. Open up. Time for your medicine."

"*No*," said the Dragon clearly and firmly.

"*No*."

*

44

"Did I hear right?" said King Keith. "Did you say *no* to the King?"

"Yes," said the Dragon. "No." And it continued to dig, scattering earth and tulips to the four winds.

"Don't be silly," said King Keith. "It's medicine to cure you. It's lovely."

He unscrewed the cap. The smell coming from the bottle was so dreadful he almost stopped breathing. The Dragon watched him suspiciously.

"Mmmm," said King Keith. "What a yummy smell. I wonder if it tastes as good as it smells."

"Only one way of finding out," said the Dragon. "Try it."

"Who, me?" gasped King Keith in horror.

"You," said the Dragon firmly, and crossed its arms.

"Just one moment," said King Keith. "A word in private."

Percy, Paula, Ludovic Linctus and King Keith went into a huddle while the Dragon returned to its digging.

"What's in this stuff?" asked King Keith suspiciously. Percy and Paula both opened their mouths to tell him. Ludovic Linctus gave them a warning look, and they closed them again.

"Oh – nothing much," said Ludovic Linctus. "This and that. That and this, and a bit of the other. It won't hurt you. In fact, it'll cure your green spots."

"I don't like the look of it,"

whispered King Keith. "Or the smell."

"You see?" said the Dragon, pausing in its digging. "He doesn't like the look of it."

"Yes I do," fibbed King Keith. "It looks lovely. It smells delicious. *Please* stop that digging and take your medicine, there's a good . . . er . . . lizard."

"You know your trouble?" said the Dragon. "You're scared."

"Don't be ridiculous," spluttered King Keith. "Gracious. Is that the time? I really must be going . . ."

"You see? said the Dragon. "He's scared to try it. He's a cowardy king."

"Oh no he's not," said Percy and Paula together. "*Are* you, Dad?"

"Why doesn't he drink it, then?"

taunted the Dragon.

"Oh all right! All right!"
screamed King Keith, finally
losing patience. "Anything to stop
you spoiling my tulips!"

And bravely, with shaking hands,
he poured the black mixture into
the spoon, took a deep breath, and
swallowed. There was a long
pause. Everyone stared at him.

"Well?" said the Dragon. "Is it
horrible?"

"Not at all," said King Keith,
crossing his fingers behind his
back. It was the worst thing he
had ever tasted in his life. A sort of
cross between dried moths, beetle
juice, fish bones, powdered
stinging nettles, chopped
toadstools and a pickled mouse
nose.

"Your turn now," he added.

"No," said the Dragon, flopping into the hole and sending showers of earth and broken tulips high into the air. "I don't like the colour."

"Why not? It's a lovely colour."

"Have some more, then," jeered the Dragon, still digging.

"Mustn't be greedy," said poor King Keith. "Somebody else."

"You," said the Dragon, peering over the edge.

"Oh – very well. If I must." And King Keith poured out another spoonful, closed his eyes and swallowed, trying very hard to think of chocolate ice cream.

"Awful, isn't it?" said the Dragon. "I know it is."

"No. I've told you, it's quite

disgus . . . delicious," spluttered King Keith bravely.

"Daddy," said Paula. "Your spots are fading!" And so they were.

"There, you see? It works," said King Keith. "Come on, Dragon. Your turn now."

"No," said the Dragon stubbornly. "I don't like the shape of the bottle."

The hole was very deep now, and the mound of earth was beginning to look like a mountain.

"Go on, Dragon," coaxed Paula. "Be brave. You want to get better, don't you?"

"I'll do if he has one more spoonful," said the Dragon. Everyone looked hopefully at King Keith.

"Oh well," he said.

"Here goes," he said.

And he took one more spoonful.

Percy, Paula and Ludovic Linctus clapped their hands. He had been so very brave.

"All right," said the Dragon in a sulky voice. "If I've *got* to."

King Keith carefully poured out a spoonful of the Dragonitus Cure. Prince Percy and Princess Paula reached into the hole and held the Dragon's nose. The huge mouth opened – and –

"Yuck! Groooooooer! Ugggy uggy ugggh!" choked the Dragon.

"Keep holding his nose!" shouted Ludovic Linctus. "He's got to have three!"

"Quite right," agreed King Keith. "After all, *I* had to. Here goes with the second!"

"Yeeeeeeeeeeeuck! Blurk.

Ooooooer," moaned the Dragon, thrashing its tail. "No more! No more!"

"Last one coming up," said King Keith. "Be brave." And down it went.

Everyone drew back with a sigh of relief. The Dragon choked, coughed and wiped its eyes.

"Look!" shouted Percy. "Its spots are fading!"

And sure enough, they were.

"I must admit I do feel much better," admitted the Dragon. "In fact, I think I'm strong enough to move away from this square now. I'm sorry about the tulips. Thanks for the medicine. It tasted awful, but it did me good. Oh well. Back to the volcano. Goodbye." And off it lumbered, doing a little skip as it went.

"Dad," said Prince Percy. "You were wonderful." And Princess Paula gave him a big kiss. "We're so proud of you," she said.

"What a stubborn creature," said King Keith, shaking his head.

"Like someone else I could mention," said Ludovic Linctus with a little smile. King Keith looked cross, then ashamed, then, finally, he laughed.

"Ludovic Linctus," he said. "You're right. I suppose I was being unreasonable. But I've certainly paid for it. That was the worst thing I've ever tasted in my life."

"I'm sorry, Your Majesty. I was in a hurry, you see. When I make some more for everybody, it'll be chocolate ice cream flavoured. If anything can hide the taste of dried moths, beetle juice, frog spawn, fish bones, chopped toadstools, a pickled mouse nose and powdered stinging nettles, it's chocolate."

King Keith went very pale. Finally, he managed a little smile. Then he gave a little wave, and began to walk away.

"Where are you going, Daddy?" called Princess Paula.

"Home to take my cold medicine," said King Keith. "After Dragonitus Cure, I can drink anything!"

And that was that.

Macaw and the Blackberry Fishcakes

John Escott

When Patsy's mum and dad took over Crab Cove's fish and chip shop, they took over Macaw as well.

Patsy, who had always wanted a pet bird, thought Macaw was beautiful with his red, yellow and blue wings and his red breast. Unfortunately, her mother did not think Macaw was quite so lovely.

"I'd have thought twice about coming if I'd known that bird was here," Mrs Forum said. "I'm sure it will cost us a fortune to keep."

Macaw had been left behind by the old owner of the shop because he was going into a rest home and couldn't take his bird with him. Rest homes had strict rules about such things.

"Isn't there a tropical bird garden we can give him to?" Mrs Forum wondered.

"SQUAW!" screamed Macaw.

"I don't think he likes that idea," Mr Forum told his wife.

"Nor do I," said Patsy, pulling a face.

So Macaw stayed, which pleased Patsy very much. And things went quite smoothly until the day of the Crab Cove Hospital Fête . . .

*

The fête began in the morning and went on all day. Patsy's mum was helping out on Mrs Hatwhistle's stall. Patsy and Macaw had gone along as well.

Macaw was perched in his favourite spot on Patsy's mop of red hair. "YARK!" he shrieked at passers-by, but in a friendly way.

Mrs Hatwhistle's stall was full of goodies. Home-made wine, home-made jam, cakes, biscuits.

"Everything looks lovely, Mrs Hatwhistle," said Patsy.

"HATWHISTLE!" screamed Macaw.

"Really, Patsy!" said Mrs Forum, looking embarrassed. "You must teach that bird some manners."

"Sorry, Mrs Hatwhistle," said Patsy.

"Bless me, dear, I don't mind,"

laughed Mrs Hatwhistle. "I think Macaw is a scream."

"SCREAM!" screamed Macaw.

"Er . . . we'll have a look round and come back later," said Patsy.

Now at this time, out in the middle of Crab Bay, there was a large white luxury yacht. It belonged to Mr Hiram J. Beefy, the American beefburger millionaire. He owned burger bars all over America and was shaped a bit like a beefburger himself.

Mr Beefy and his wife, Lydia, were on a world cruise.

"What a darling little place," Mrs Beefy said when she saw Crab Cove. She was as thin as a stick insect, which made people laugh when they heard her married name.

Hiram J. sighed. "Yes, honey."
He was bored with cruising.
Getting ideas to improve his
burger bars was what interested
him, and he didn't think Crab Cove
would provide him with any of
those.

But he was wrong.

Back at the fête, Macaw had taken
off from Patsy's hair (which he had

got into the habit of using as a landing pad) and flown over to Mrs Hatwhistle's stall again. He seemed especially interested in a bottle of wine that hung in a basket under the canopy of the stall.

"Blackberry Wine – only £1.50," it said on the label.

"SQUAW!" said Macaw – and he picked up the basket by the handle and flew off with it, over the heads of the crowd.

"Macaw!" cried Mrs Forum. "Bring that back at once."

Macaw didn't even look round.

A few minutes later, when Patsy arrived back carrying a large chocolate ice cream, she could see something was wrong by the look on her mother's face.

"Where's Macaw?" she said.

"That *bird*!" shouted Mrs Forum.

In fact, Macaw had taken his prize home. He flew into the kitchen at the back of Forum's Fish Parlour and perched on a shelf above the worktop.

Then, slowly, he pecked the cork from the bottle of wine, the neck hanging over the edge of the shelf . . .

. . . And the wine poured steadily downwards – straight into a large bowl which stood on the worktop. In the bowl was a fishy mixture.

Macaw lost interest in the bottle after the wine had stopped gurgling and he flew out of the window in search of some new adventure.

The fishy mixture gradually
changed colour.

Several minutes later, Mr Forum
returned to his kitchen after
answering the phone. "Now what
was I doing?" he said to himself.
"Ah, yes. The fishcake mix." And
he went over to the large bowl on
the worktop and began stirring it.
He didn't notice that the fishcake

mix had more of a pinky tinge to it now.

Out on Hiram J. Beefy's yacht, the millionaire and his wife were having a late breakfast. Mrs Beefy was eating a grapefruit, while her husband tucked into a king-sized beefburger of the sort that had made him his fortune.

Suddenly, there was a flapping sound, and they both turned to see Macaw landing on the rail of the yacht.

"Look, honey," said Hiram J. "It's a macaw!"

Lydia looked tickled pink. "I wonder if it talks?" she said.

She didn't have to wonder long.

"PIE-AND-CHIPS-CHICKEN-AND-CHIPS-PEA-FRITTERS-FISHCAKES-

PASS-THE-VINEGAR!" screamed Macaw.

Hiram J. stared in astonishment. "Did you hear that, Lydia? He's telling you what is on the menu at some restaurant. Now that's what I call smart. A flying advertisement!"

"WHERE'S-THE-SALT?" shrieked Macaw, and flew off towards Crab Cove.

Hiram J. Beefy forgot about his breakfast. "I have to find out where he's going. I've never tasted a pea-fritter. Who knows, maybe it's something I can introduce into the burger bars?"

And he called for one of his crew to launch the small boat.

Patsy had arrived back at the shop in time for the midday opening.

Because Mrs Forum was staying at the fête, Patsy was to act as waitress at the four tables in Forum's Fish Parlour. But she was worried about Macaw.

Patsy told her father what the bird had done at the fête.

"Dear me," was all that Mr Forum said.

At that moment, Macaw flew past the window and perched on the hanging sign outside the shop.

"There he is!" cried Patsy.

"He's not carrying any bottles of wine," Mr Forum observed.

"Oh dear," said Patsy. "I wonder what he's done with it."

Just then, a large man in expensive yachting clothes came into the shop and collapsed into a chair at one of the tables. He had

obviously been running. "Is that
. . . your bird?" he gasped, nodding
to Macaw outside.

"Er . . . yes," Patsy admitted,
wondering what Macaw had been
up to now.

But the man just gave a nod and
said, "Good". Without looking at
the menu, he said, "I'll have two
pea-fritters, two fishcakes and
some chips, please."

"Yes, sir," said Patsy, one eye on
Macaw.

"YESSIR!" said Macaw through
the open window.

The American stayed right
through lunchtime. He ate what he
had ordered, then he asked Patsy
to bring him some more of "those
delicious fishcakes".

"He's got an enormous

appetite," Patsy whispered to her father.

"It's very strange," said Mr Forum, "but several customers have come back for more fishcakes today. They're all saying how nice they are. It's a good job I made an extra-large helping of mixture."

It was much later, when Patsy was busy clearing up in the kitchen, that she glanced up and saw the empty wine bottle on the shelf.

"So *that's* where it got to," she said. Then she noticed the empty bowl on the worktop beneath it. "Oh, my goodness. Dad!" she called.

Mr Forum came into the kitchen.

"Uh . . . your fishcakes," she said. "Did you mix them in that?" Patsy nodded to the bowl beneath the empty wine bottle.

"Yes," said Mr Forum. "Why?"

Patsy pointed to the empty wine bottle. "I . . . er . . . think you had something extra in today's mix."

Mr Forum looked up at the bottle. "Whatever . . . ?"

"Mrs Hatwhistle's blackberry wine," said Patsy.

"Oh!" said Mr Forum.

Later, when the shop was closing for the afternoon, Hiram J. Beefy went over to the counter to speak to Mr Forum and Patsy.

"Sir," he said. "I'd like to congratulate you on a most original dish."

"You would?" said Mr Forum, looking surprised.

The American nodded. "I'm talking about your fishcakes. I've never tasted any like them before. You must have your own special recipe."

"Well . . ." began Mr Forum.

Hiram J. held up a hand. "Now I don't expect you to tell me your recipe for nothing. What do you say to a thousand dollars?"

Mr Forum blinked in astonishment. Patsy's mouth fell open.

"Oh . . . well, really . . . I couldn't . . ." Mr Forum began.

"Nonsense," said Hiram J. "I insist on paying you something. I want to make and sell them in my burger bars in America."

"But – but it was an accident," said Mr Forum.

Now it was Hiram J. Beefy's turn to look surprised. "Accident?"

Mr Forum explained about Macaw and the bottle of wine. "And so what you had this morning," he finished, "were *blackberry* fishcakes. A sort of *freak* fishcake."

Hiram J. began to laugh. "Let's get this straight," he chuckled. "It's a normal fishcake mix, plus one bottle of blackberry wine?" And he laughed and laughed.

Patsy and Mr Forum laughed with him.

In the end, because Mr Forum wouldn't take any money, the millionaire made a generous donation to the hospital fête fund. And Mr Forum told him how to make pea-fritters, free of charge, so Hiram J. Beefy went away a very happy man.

'Wait until we tell Mum," said Patsy, after the American had gone. "She'll have to let Macaw stay now. Blackberry fishcakes could make us millionaires like Mr Beefy."

"Well, we've already sold more than three times the number we usually do," he agreed. "We must tell Mrs Hatwhistle. After all, it was her blackberry wine that did the trick. We'll have to go into business together. The Hatwhistle and Forum Blackberry Fishcake Company!" Mr Forum laughed.

"BLACKBERRY FISHCAKES!" screamed Macaw, automatically adding an extra item to his

71

squawk-aloud menu. "BLACKBERRY
FISHCAKES!"

And after that day, they became
a regular feature at Forum's Fish
Parlour.

Josie Smith and the Concert

Magdalen Nabb

"**W**e're having a concert!" shouted Josie Smith, running in from school and banging the door.

"Don't bang the door," said Josie's mum. "How many times have I told you?"

"I forgot," said Josie Smith. "Mum, we're having a concert at school and our class is doing a play and we're all in it!"

"Don't shout," said Josie's mum. "I can hear you."

"We're going to be fairies," said Josie Smith, "and the boys are being elves and there's a fairy queen and a fairy king and another thing that I've forgotten and Tahara's going to be it. Mum?"

"What?"

"When will my hair be as long as Tahara's?"

"It takes years and years for hair to grow as long as Tahara's."

"As long as Eileen's, then?"

"I don't know. What's happened to your ribbon?"

Josie Smith felt her tiny plait. "I've lost it," she said.

"Again!" said Josie's mum. "Go and wash your hands. You're filthy."

"I want to tell you about the

concert," said Josie Smith.

"You can tell me while you wash your hands," said Josie's mum.

"We're having frocks made of crêpe paper," said Josie Smith, "and paper flowers in our hair and the boys are having paper hats with pointed ears stuck on. Will you make my costume?"

"I'll probably end up making more than just yours," said Josie's mum, "if it's anything like last year's nativity play."

"That's because you're good at sewing," said Josie Smith. "Mum? I'm hungry and thirsty."

"Well, help me to set the table, then."

Josie Smith helped.

After tea she went next door to Eileen's and played.

Eileen said: "My mum's buying all the crêpe paper for all the costumes and some flowers for the stage. Only, you haven't to tell anybody because it's a secret."

The next day, at school, they practised one of their songs for the concert. They practised in the hall after dinner while the dinner ladies were stacking the tables and everything smelled of cabbage and the windows were steamed up because it was raining.

All the girls wanted Miss Valentine to say who was going to be the fairy queen but Miss Valentine said, "I haven't decided yet."

At playtime, a girl called Ann Lomax came up and whispered to Josie Smith. "Do you want to know a secret?" she said.

"Yes," said Josie Smith.

Ann Lomax wasn't Josie Smith's friend. She sat at another table. She had a kilt like Josie Smith's, only yellow, and she had blond hair and sometimes she had specks of red on her nails because her mum let her play with nail varnish at home.

Ann Lomax put her hands round her mouth and whispered hard in Josie Smith's ear and made it feel hot.

"You won't tell?" she whispered.

"No," said Josie Smith.

"Eileen's mum came to school at dinner time."

"Well?" said Josie Smith.

"Sh! You haven't to tell anybody! She brought some stuff for the concert and one of the dinner ladies heard her say, 'If our Eileen's not the fairy queen there'll be trouble.'"

And Ann Lomax ran away.

Josie Smith played with Eileen. When the whistle went and they were lining up, Eileen whispered to Josie Smith, "It's between you and me who's going to be the queen, my mum said."

The next day at dinner time it was raining again when they practised their song in the hall. The big windows were all steamed up and everything smelled of stew. When they'd finished singing, Miss Valentine made them all go up on the stage and stand in a line.

"Boys on this side and girls on that side," she said.

Then she looked at them all and said: "Who's the tallest of you boys?"

The boys all said: "Rawley Baxter!"

"And who's the tallest girl?"

The girls all said: "Julie Horrocks!"

"Rawley Baxter and Julie Horrocks, come and stand in the middle," said Miss Valentine.

Rawley Baxter and Julie Horrocks stood in the middle and Miss Valentine said, "Because you're the tallest, you're going to be the fairy king and queen."

Rawley Baxter said, "I don't want to."

Julie Horrocks didn't say anything. She had long thin legs and big glasses and a fringe and she was taller than Rawley Baxter.

"She doesn't look like a fairy queen," whispered Eileen. "And anyway, she's ugly because she's got glasses."

"All the fairies stand in a circle around the fairy queen," said Miss Valentine, "and now, sit down on the floor."

When they were sitting down, Eileen whispered to Josie Smith, "And anyway, when we did the nativity play in the baby class, Julie Horrocks wet her knickers and the angel next to her slipped in the puddle."

Josie Smith didn't say anything. She pointed at the fairy king when Miss Valentine said to point, and she sang. She liked being a fairy.

At home time, Eileen said, "I'm

telling my mum I don't want to be in the concert."

Josie Smith ran in at her own front door.

"Mum!" she shouted, "Julie Horrocks is being the fairy queen because she's the tallest, and she's got a fringe and glasses."

"Wash your hands," said Josie's mum, "and your face, while I finish sewing this seam. I don't know how you manage to get so filthy at school."

"We had to sit on the floor," said Josie Smith, "when we were practising our play for the concert."

"What's it about?" asked Josie's mum.

"I don't know," said Josie Smith. "We have to point at the fairy king and sing a song. Mum, Julie Horrocks is the queen and she hasn't even got blond curly hair like Eileen."

Josie's mum put her sewing away and started cooking something.

"Are you upset because you're not the queen?" she asked.

"No," said Josie Smith. "I like being a fairy." But then she said, "I wish I had a fringe like Julie Horrocks."

"I thought you wanted to grow your hair like Tahara's," said Josie's mum.

"I do," said Josie Smith, "but I want a fringe, as well."

"It could do with cutting," said Josie's mum, and she stroked Josie Smith's hair. "It's so untidy. If you really want to grow it we should trim it all to the same length and then it'll grow nicely."

"And cut me a fringe?" asked Josie Smith.

"All right," said Josie's mum.

So, after tea, Josie Smith sat on a chair in front of the fire with a towel tucked round her neck and newspapers round her feet, and her mum cut her hair.

Snick, snick, snick, went Josie's mum round the back of her neck.

"It tickles," said Josie Smith.

"Keep still."

Snick, snick, snick, went Josie's mum round her ears.

"Mum," said Josie Smith, "Julie Horrocks wet her knickers on the stage when we were in the baby class."

"I know she did. I remember."

"And then she cried, didn't she? She cries when we have a spelling test, as well."

"She's very highly strung," said Josie's mum.

"Is that why her legs are so long?" asked Josie Smith, "and she never plays out?"

"She's shy because she's so tall," said Josie's mum. "You should call for her sometimes."

"I did call for her," said Josie Smith, "and she wouldn't play out and we went in her bedroom and she keeps all her toys in a line on the shelf and she doesn't play with them. When are you going to cut my fringe?"

"In a minute. Keep still."

"Do you want me to sing you the song that we're practising at school?"

"If you want, only keep your head still."

"I am keeping it still," said Josie Smith, and then she sang:

"You spo-otte-ed snakes with dou-ou-bl-le tongues,

"Thorn-y hedgehogs co-ome not near!"

Snick, went Josie's mum, *snick, snick, snick*.

"Come not near our fairy queen!" sang Josie Smith.

Snick, went Josie's mum, *snick, snick, snick*.

"Lulla-lulla-lulla-by," sang Josie Smith.

Snick, went Josie's mum, *snick, snick, snick*.

"I can't remember any more," said Josie Smith.

"Keep really still, now," said Josie's mum, "and shut your eyes." And the cold scissors went nipping across Josie Smith's forehead making a little fringe. *Snick, snick, snick*.

When she'd finished, the newspapers on the floor round Josie Smith's chair had little snips of hair all over them. Josie's mum threw the snips of hair in the fire

and they sizzled. Then she let
Josie Smith stand on the chair to
look in the mirror. Josie Smith
smiled.

"I like my fringe," she said. "Can
I have a curl in it?"

"No," said Josie's mum. "You'll
never get to sleep with a roller in
your hair. It'll hurt you."

"But for the concert, can I?"

"All right," said Josie's mum.
"Just for the concert. Now, get
ready for bed."

Josie Smith got ready for bed,
and in the bathroom she stood on
the stool to look in the mirror
again and see if her fringe was still
there, and she smiled. When she
was in bed and her mum had
switched the light off and gone
down, she felt for her fringe in the

dark. It was nice and smooth. "I've got a fringe," she whispered to Ginger in his basket by the bed.

"Eeiow," said Ginger.

Josie Smith sang a bit of her song for Ginger very quietly in the dark. Ginger purred. When she couldn't remember any more, Josie Smith and Ginger fell asleep.

In the morning, when Eileen came to call for her to go to school, Josie Smith said: "I've got a fringe."

"It's short, your hair," Eileen said. "It makes you look like a boy."

"It doesn't," said Josie Smith, "and anyway, when it's the concert I'm having curls."

At dinner time, when they practised in the hall, it was

raining hard again and they had to have the lights on. The big windows were all steamed up and everything smelled of fish. After the song they went up on the stage and Miss Valentine said, "Today, you're going to learn a little dance. First of all, divide into pairs, a fairy and an elf to each pair."

They all started arguing and pushing and making a terrible noise and then Miss Potts came marching into the hall and shouted. She stopped with her hands on her hips and her face all red and said, "You children are making far too much noise! I can hear the row you're making from my office!"

Miss Valentine said quietly,

"Come on, now, make your pairs. It doesn't matter who you choose, you can always change later."

But the children all shouted: "Miss Valentine, there aren't enough elves!"

"Oh dear," said Miss Valentine, "There are two boys away."

And the children all shouted: "Miss Valentine, and they're having their tonsils out and they won't be back for the concert!"

And they all started arguing and pushing again.

"Will you be quiet!" roared Miss Potts, and she stamped onto the stage shouting, "I'll see to this, Miss Valentine!"

And she started pushing the children about, roaring: "Stand still! Go over there! You come to the front where we can see you! Be quiet!" Then she shouted: "Eileen, stand here! Now, Josie Smith, come to me! You've got the shortest hair of all the girls so you can be an elf! Come and stand here next to Eileen!"

Josie Smith went. Her chest was going *bam, bam, bam*, but she didn't say anything. She was frightened of Miss Potts.

Miss Potts stamped down off the stage, shouting, "A lot of fuss about nothing! And don't let me hear this class making a noise again! Practise quietly!" And she marched away.

Josie Smith stood next to Eileen with her chest going *bam, bam, bam*, and her face all hot, waiting for Miss Valentine to send her

back to her own side to be a fairy.
But Miss Valentine didn't say
anything. She wasn't smiling like
she usually did and nobody liked
practising any more. Everybody
did the dance wrong and Josie
Smith couldn't even sing any more
because she had a big lump in her
throat.

In the afternoon, instead of a
story, Miss Valentine told them
about the play. She said that
Tahara was a child stolen by the
queen from the prince of a faraway
land and changed into a fairy and
that she wouldn't need a costume
because she could wear one of her
own beautiful dresses with golden
stripes and trousers underneath,
because Tahara came from a
faraway land like the stolen child.

She said that the fairies would
dance in their bare feet and have
paper flowers on their hands as
well as in their hair and that the
elves, as well as having paper hats
and tunics, had to wear woolly
tights borrowed from their sisters
or mums.

When they were putting their
coats on at home time, Miss
Valentine came and put her hand
on Josie Smith's head and stroked
her fringe and said, "Thank you
for being an elf, Josie. The dance
will look much nicer with the
same number of elves and fairies.
You don't mind not being a fairy,
do you?"

"No," said Josie Smith, shutting
her eyes tight because it was a lie.

Out in the yard, Eileen and Ann

Lomax pulled Josie Smith's fringe and said, "Josie Smith's a boy! Josie Smith's a boy!"

Josie Smith put her head down and ran as fast as her wellingtons would go down the street and in at her own front door.

"What's the matter with you?" said Josie's mum. "You're all red in the face."

"I don't like Miss Valentine any more," said Josie Smith.

"Has she been shouting at you?" said Josie's mum.

"No," said Josie Smith.

"Run across to Mrs Chadwick's for me," said Josie's mum, "and get a quarter of boiled ham for tea, there's a good girl. And afterwards you can help me with the fairies' costumes."

"I don't want to," said Josie Smith.

"I'm going to make some tiny flowers with loops to fit on their fingers," said Josie's mum. "You'll like doing that."

Josie Smith didn't say anything. She ran across to Mrs Chadwick's for the boiled ham and after tea she helped her mum with the paper flowers. She didn't want to tell her mum that she wasn't being a fairy any more. She didn't even tell Ginger at bedtime. She didn't want to tell anybody. She lay in bed in the dark and pulled and pulled at her short hair until it hurt so much that she cried, and she hated her mum for cutting it.

On the last day before the concert there were people

practising in the hall all day. Josie Smith could hear the piano from her classroom when she was doing her sums, and when she was reading she could hear another class saying a poem all together, Josie Smith's class had to practise after dinner. Josie Smith's mum and some other mums were bringing all the costumes to try on.

When it was time, they lined up and Miss Valentine took them into the hall. The wall at the back of the stage was all covered over with black crêpe paper with stars and a moon stuck on. Josie Smith's chest went *bam, bam, bam*, because, even if she couldn't be a fairy, she was still excited because of the concert. Everybody else was

excited, too, and when they
started to get undressed they were
all falling over each other and
pushing and giggling and losing
their clothes and Miss Valentine
couldn't keep them quiet. Josie
Smith didn't get ready. She didn't
want to. She looked at the table
where the fairies' dresses were and
saw a heap of big paper flowers
and a heap of small ones, yellow
and white and purple. But then
somebody's mum got hold of Josie
Smith and started undressing her
and somebody else's mum tried a
paper hat on her with a pointy top
and pointy paper ears stuck on the
sides and pulled it right down over
her fringe. Then she smiled and
said, "You do look a comic."

Josie Smith went in a corner at

the back near the stage. She sat down with her legs crossed and started crying. At first she tried not to make any noise so that nobody would notice, but then she cried louder and louder because she couldn't help it and nobody noticed anyway because they were all shouting and talking and pushing and arguing and losing their shoes and ripping their paper costumes. Even Josie's mum didn't notice. But all of a sudden a loud voice said:

"Who's that crying?"

Josie Smith pulled the elf's hat further down over her fringe and put her head down on her knees with her eyes shut. Everybody stopped shouting and pushing and stood still to listen. Josie Smith

listened, too, but she didn't hear anybody say, "Josie Smith's crying." Instead, she heard a boy's voice roaring.

"Wa-a-a-a-a-ah! Wa-a-a-a-a-ah! Wa-a-a-a-a-ah!"

And then somebody said, "It's Rawley Baxter!"

Josie Smith opened her eyes. Everybody was staring at Rawley

Baxter. He was standing in the middle of the hall in woolly tights and a green paper cloak and a gold paper crown with his eyes shut tight and his mouth wide open, roaring.

"Wa-a-a-a-a-ah! Wa-a-a-a-a-ah! Wa-a-a-a-a-ah!" roared Rawley Baxter. "Wa-a-a-a-a-ah! Wa-a-a-a-a-ah! Wa-a-a-a-a-ah!"

Miss Valentine said, "Whatever's the matter?"

She went and put her arm round him but Rawley Baxter pushed her away and then slapped and whacked at his green paper cloak, trying to get it off, and roaring, "Wa-a-a-a-a-ah! Wa-a-a-a-a-ah! Wa-a-a-a-a-ah!"

"Tell me, what's the matter?" said Miss Valentine.

But Rawley Baxter wouldn't tell.

Ann Lomax knew what was the matter and she told.

"Miss Valentine, he doesn't want to be a fairy king because it's soft. Miss Valentine, he only likes being Batman and he doesn't want to be dressed up in a green cloak."

"Oh dear," said Miss Valentine, but before she could do anything about it, the children all shouted:

"Miss Valentine! Miss Valentine! Julie Horrocks is crying, as well!"

Everybody looked at Julie Horrocks. She was standing on the stage in her white paper frock and her big glasses and her long thin legs, going, "Ooomp! Ooomp! Ooomp!" and big tears were rolling down her face.

101

"Whatever's the matter?" asked Miss Valentine.

"Ooomp!" said Julie Horrocks. "Ooomp! Ooomp! Ooomp!" and she wouldn't tell.

Ann Lomax knew what was the matter and she told.

"Miss Valentine, it's because she's got to stand at the front because she's the queen and everybody will see that she's too tall so she wants to stand at the back and be an ordinary fairy."

"Oomp!" sobbed Julie Horrocks. "Ooomp! Ooomp! Ooomp!"

"Wa-a-a-a-a-a-ah!" roared Rawley Baxter. "Wa-a-a-a-a-a-ah! Wa-a-a-a-a-a-ah! Wa-a-a-a-a-a-ah!"

"Oh dear," said Miss Valentine, but before she could do anything about it, all the children shouted:

"Miss Valentine! Miss Valentine! Eileen's crying as well!"

Everybody looked at Eileen. She was leaning against the wall with her face in her hands, going: "Meh-heh-heh! Meh-heh-heh! Meh-heh-heh!" as loud as she could.

"What's the matter with you?" said Miss Valentine.

"Meh-heh-heh!" wailed Eileen. "Meh-heh-heh! Meh-heh-heh! Meh-heh-heh" and she wouldn't tell.

Ann Lomax knew and she told.

"Miss Valentine, it's because she wants to be the fairy queen, her mum promised her she would be, because she's got golden curls."

"Meh-heh-heh!" wailed Eileen against the wall. "Meh-heh-heh! Meh-heh-heh! Meh-heh-heh!"

"Oomp!" sobbed Julie Horrocks on the stage. "Ooomp! Ooomp! Ooomp!"

"Wa-a-a-a-a-a-ah!" roared Rawley Baxter in the middle of the hall. "Wa-a-a-a-a-a-ah! Wa-a-a-a-a-a-ah! Wa-a-a-a-a-a-ah!"

"Oh dear," said Miss Valentine, but before she could do anything about it, all the children shouted:

"Miss Valentine! Miss Valentine! Tahara's crying as well."

Everybody looked at Tahara.

Tahara was in the middle of all the fairies, wearing her fire-coloured frock and trousers with golden stripes. She hardly made any noise at all but tears were rolling down her face from her big black eyes and every so often she went: "Nff! Nff! Nff!"

"Tahara," said Miss Valentine. "Whatever's the matter with you?"

"Nff!" went Tahara quietly. "Nff! Nff! Nff!" and she wouldn't tell.

Ann Lomax knew and she told.

"Miss Valentine, it's because she has to wear her own frock and she wants a paper costume like Josie Smith."

"Nff!" sniffed Tahara in the middle of the fairies. "Nff! Nff! Nff!"

"Meh-heh-heh!" wailed Eileen against the wall. "Meh-heh-heh! Meh-heh-heh! Meh-heh-heh!"

"Oooomp!" sobbed Julie Horrocks on the stage. "Oooomp! Oooomp! Oooomp!"

"Wa-a-a-a-a-a-ah!" roared Rawley Baxter in the middle of the hall.

"Wa-a-a-a-a-a-ah! Wa-a-a-a-a-a-ah! Wa-a-a-a-a-ah!"

Josie Smith cried a bit harder to join in but nobody noticed her in her corner on the floor.

"Oh dear," said Miss Valentine.

Then Josie's mum went up to Rawley Baxter.

Wa-a-a-a-a-a-ah!" roared Rawley Baxter.

"Listen," said Josie's mum.

"Wa-a-a-a-a-a-ah!" said Rawley Baxter.

"Listen," said Josie's mum, and she took the green cloak off him. "We've got some black crêpe paper left over from the sky. If you want I'll make you a black cloak and afterwards you can use it to be Batman."

Rawley Baxter stopped crying.

"Can I wear my Batman mask with the cloak in the concert as well?" he said.

Josie's mum looked at Miss Valentine.

"All right," said Miss Valentine, "as long as he wears the gold crown, too."

Rawley Baxter smiled.

Then Josie's mum went up on the stage.

"Oooomp!" said Julie Horrocks.

"Listen," said Josie's mum.

"Oooomp!" said Julie Horrocks.

"Listen," said Josie's mum. "You don't have to be the fairy queen if you're too frightened, does she, Miss Valentine?"

"I suppose not," said Miss Valentine.

Julie Horrocks stopped crying.

"You can be a fairy," said Josie's mum, "and stand near the back where nobody can see your legs."

Julie Horrocks smiled.

"Give me your crown," said Josie's mum, and she came down off the stage and went over to Eileen.

"Meh-heh-heh!" said Eileen.

"Listen," said Josie's mum.

"Meh-heh-heh!" said Eileen.

"Listen" said Josie's mum. "Julie Horrocks doesn't want to be the queen any more and I'm sure if you stop crying Miss Valentine will let you be the queen instead, won't you, Miss Valentine?"

"All right," said Miss Valentine.

Eileen stopped crying.

"Look," said Josie's mum. "Here's your silver crown. You can change into the white frock afterwards." And she put the silver crown on Eileen's golden curls.

Eileen smiled.

"Now," said Josie's mum. "What are we going to do about Tahara?"

"Nff!" said Tahara.

"What do you want to be?" asked Josie's mum.

"Nff!" said Tahara.

"She doesn't want to wear her own frock," Ann Lomax said.

"Does anybody else want to wear Tahara's frock?" asked Josie's mum.

"I do," Ann Lomax said.

"And what does Miss Valentine say?" asked Josie's mum.

"I wanted Tahara to be the stolen child," Miss Valentine said, "because she's supposed to be dark

and come from a faraway land."
But then she said, "Oh dear. All
right."

"I can put make-up on," Ann
Lomax said. "My mum lets me
sometimes."

"All right," Miss Valentine said,
and Josie's mum took Tahara's
frock off her and gave it to Ann
Lomax.

Ann Lomax smiled.

"What do you want to wear,
Tahara?" asked Josie's mum.

Tahara pointed and everybody
looked where she was pointing.

She was pointing at Josie Smith
in her elf's hat, sitting cross-
legged in the corner.

"Josie," said Josie's mum. "Come
here a minute, will you?"

Josie came. She wasn't crying any

more now that nobody else was.

"I didn't know you were being an elf," said Josie's mum. "But now Tahara wants your costume. Will you let her wear it?"

"Yes," said Josie Smith.

"You can wear Ann Lomax's fairy costume" said Josie's mum.

"Yes," said Josie Smith, and she took off her elf's hat and gave it to Tahara.

Tahara smiled. Then she stroked the paper ears.

"Here you are," said Josie's mum, and she gave Josie Smith the flowers for her hair and fingers.

Josie Smith smiled.

"Has everybody stopped crying?" asked Miss Valentine.

"Yes!" shouted all the children.

"Well, thank goodness for that,"

said Miss Valentine.

And the next night when all the mums and dads were in their seats in the hall and Josie Smith was waiting to go on the stage with her fairy frock and flowers and a curl in her fringe, Miss Valentine came and put her arm round her and said, "I wanted to say thank you to you, Josie, for not being selfish. I don't think you really liked being an elf, did you?"

"No," said Josie Smith.

"But you didn't make a fuss and cry like Eileen and the others did."

"No," said Josie Smith with her eyes half shut.

"I don't know how I would have managed," Miss Valentine said, "without you and your mum. All right, are you ready to go on?"

"Yes," said Josie Smith, pointing her toe and holding her paper skirt out with flowery fingers.

"Shh!" said Miss Valentine to all the elves and fairies. "It's time!"

When they went on the stage they all waved to their mums and dads and Josie Smith waved to her mum and her gran and then they remembered to sing.

Josie Smith felt so shiny and happy that she sang twice as loud as she'd ever sung before.

"Come not near our fairy queen!" she sang, and Eileen lay down to sleep with her eyes shut tight and the silver crown on her golden curls.

"Lul-la-by," sang Josie Smith, "lul-la-by! Lul-lu-la-by!"

Dilly and the Horror Film

Tony Bradman

*Dilly is a young dinosaur who lives
with his parents and his sister
Dorla. Dilly is always finding
himself in trouble and when he
does he tends to let rip with a 150-
mile-per-hour, ultra-special super-
scream!*

I like watching TV, don't you?
My favourite programme is
Dinosaur Street. I don't watch
scary programmes, though. I don't
like them at all.

I don't watch as much TV as Dilly, either. Mother says that he's got square eyes because he watches so much TV, and he's always trying to watch more. The other morning, for instance, he wanted to turn on the TV straight after breakfast.

"That's not a very good idea, Dilly," said Father. "It's a lovely day, so why don't you play outside instead?"

"I don't want to play outside," said Dilly, with a sulky look. "I want to watch the cartoons on TV."

"Now, now, Dilly," said Father. "What you *want* and what you *get* might be two very different things. What do you think you'll get if you don't say please?"

"I'll get what I want," said Dilly, who was looking even more sulky.

"Oh no you won't," said Father. I could see that Dilly had made him cross.

"Little dinosaurs who don't say please get sent to their rooms. And if they don't behave, they aren't allowed to watch TV at all, not even the *D-Team* or *Dinosaur Attack!*"

That evening, Mother and Father were going out to a party. We didn't mind, though, because that meant Grandmother was coming to babysit, and that's always fun. Grandmother usually lets us stay up a little later than we should, and she tells us really funny stories about when Father was a naughty little dinosaur.

Grandmother arrived, and Mother and Father went out soon afterwards.

"Bye," they said. "Be good, you two!"

Grandmother gave us something to eat, and then we watched TV for a while.

"You really like watching TV, don't you, Dilly?" said Grandmother. Dilly just nodded without taking his eyes off the screen.

"You must take after your father, then," said Grandmother. "If your grandfather and I had let him, he would have watched TV all the time when he was your age."

Dilly looked round at Grandmother.

"Would he really, Grandmother?" he said.

"Oh yes," she said. She laughed, and shook her head. "He was so bad, your father, sometimes. I remember once that he sneaked down very late at night just to watch TV. Grandfather and I were in bed, and we thought he was asleep . . . but we heard the noise of the TV, and came down and caught him. He got such a telling off . . . and that was the last time he ever did anything like that!"

I could see that Dilly looked very interested in what Grandmother was saying.

Grandmother told us lots more stories about Father when he was little, and then suddenly she looked up at the clock.

"I didn't realize how late it was," she said. "Come along, you two, I'd better get you into bed, or your mother and father will want to tell *me* off when they get home."

"But I want to watch more TV, Grandmother," said Dilly.

"Well, Dilly," said Grandmother, "I'm afraid you can't. It's time for you to have a bath and go to bed, and besides, there's nothing on the TV for you now. At this time of the evening it's all programmes for grown-ups."

"But why can't I watch programmes for grown-ups? I want to," said Dilly. Grandmother sighed.

"That's hard to explain, Dilly," she said. "But I'm sure you'd think most of them were just boring, and some of them might frighten you."

"But . . ." Dilly started to say.

"No more buts, Dilly," said Grandmother, who was beginning to look cross. "It's time for bed!"

I thought for a moment that Dilly was going to be naughty and argue, but he didn't. He had a strange look on his face, though, as if he was planning something . . .

Grandmother took us upstairs to get ready for bed. Dilly was very well-behaved. He didn't use too much toothpaste, and he got into his pyjamas without any fuss at all.

Grandmother said she would read us some stories next. I asked if we could have some from my favourite book, *Fairy Tales for Young Dinosaurs*. Grandmother read two stories . . . and then she started to yawn, great big, tired yawns.

"Oh dear," she said. "I don't know why, but that last story's made me really sleepy. I think you've had enough stories now, anyway, you two. It's time you went to sleep."

Grandmother tucked us up in our beds, kissed us, and went off downstairs, still yawning.

"Goodnight, Dorla and . . . *yawwwn* . . . Dilly."

"Goodnight, Grandmother," said Dilly and I. And then I snuggled down in my bed and started going to sleep. I was quite tired, so it wasn't long before I was dreaming away.

But I didn't *stay* asleep. I remember that I was having a

dream about someone screaming. The next minute I was awake, and I could hear someone screaming for real.

And then I realized what it was, or rather *who* it was. It was Dilly, and he was letting rip with a 150-mile-per-hour, ultra-special super-scream, and it was so loud that it had woken me up, even though it was coming from downstairs. I got out of bed and went to see what was going on.

By the time I got downstairs, Dilly had stopped screaming. I could hear Grandmother talking to him.

"There, there, Dilly," she was saying, "it's all right. It's only a TV programme . . . but you're such a naughty dinosaur."

I opened the door and peeped round. Grandmother was sitting on the sofa hugging Dilly who was crying. Grandmother saw me and called me in.

"Quick, Dorla," she said. "Turn off the TV."

Grandmother didn't have to ask me to do that twice. I could see that there was a really scary programme on, a film that was meant only for grown-up dinosaurs. There were some horrible monsters in it doing nasty things, two-legged monsters with smooth skins and hairy heads. I found out later that it was called *Invasion of the Humans*, and I hope I never see anything like it again.

Grandmother calmed Dilly

down, and then got him back into bed. When she tucked me in again, she explained that she had fallen asleep in front of the TV.

"Dilly must have sneaked down," she said, "seen that I was asleep, and switched channels. I woke up after a while because the film was so noisy, and touched Dilly on the shoulder. He must have thought

that I was a monster come to get him, because he screamed and screamed and screamed."

Grandmother gave me a kiss, and went back to see if Dilly was all right.

In the morning, at breakfast, Dilly was very quiet. It turned out that he had woken up again in the night after Mother and Father had come home. He had been having a terrible nightmare about two-legged monsters with hairy heads.

"Grandmother's told us all about last night, Dilly," said Father. "But I'm not going to tell you off because I think you've learned your lesson. Do you promise you won't do it again?"

"I promise, Father," said Dilly.

And when Grandmother came to

babysit again, she told us that she'd had nightmares every night for a week after the last time.

"I had nightmares too, Grandmother," said Dilly, "all about horrible monsters."

"Oh, my nightmares weren't about monsters, Dilly," she said. "They were about horrible little dinosaurs who scream and don't do what they're told. And they all looked like you."

And we all laughed – even Dilly!

Trouble in the Supermarket

Margaret Mahy

One day when he was in a very joking mood Mr Delmonico offended a word witch. He did it by being a bit too clever. (Too much cleverness is often offensive to witches.)

Mr Delmonico, with his twins, Francis and Sarah, was shopping at the supermarket. The witch was there too, pushing a shopping trolley and talking to herself as word witches do . . . they need a lot of words going on around them all the time.

"I'll have some peanut butter," she said.

"You'd butter not," cried Mr Delmonico, laughing at his own joke. The word witch took no notice, just went on talking to herself.

"And then perhaps I'll have a loaf of wholemeal bread," she went on.

Mr Delmonico winked at the twins. "How can you make a meal out of a hole?" he asked. "It doesn't sound very nice."

Francis and Sarah were horrified to hear their father speaking so carelessly to a word witch. But the witch ignored him. She was trying hard to behave well in a public place.

"I'll get some beans," she muttered.

Mr Delmonico looked at the beans. He couldn't resist another joke. "They look more like 'might-have-beans'," he remarked with a smile.

Now the witch turned on him, glaring with her small red eyes. "I've had quite enough of you," she cried. "You shall suffer from whirling words and see how you like it."

Mr Delmonico was suddenly serious as the word witch scuttled away.

Whirling words sounded as if they might be painful.

"I'm afraid I might have got us into a bit of a jam," he said to the twins.

"Daddy, be careful!" cried Sarah, but it was too late. They were up to their ankles in several kinds of jam. Francis was mainly mixed up with strawberry, Sarah with plum and apple, while Mr Delmonico himself had melon and ginger jam up over the turn-ups of his trousers. The manager of the supermarket came hurrying up.

"What's going on here?" he cried.

"Nothing really," Mr Delmonico said, trying to sound casual. "Just some jam that was lying around."

"There's something fishy about this," declared the manager and then gasped, for a large flapping fish appeared out of nowhere and struck him on the right ear. Sarah and Francis realized that anyone near Mr Delmonico was going to suffer from whirling words too.

"You are to blame for all this mess," said the manager, "and you'll have to pay for it."

"Oh, will I!" replied Mr Delmonico, trying hard to keep calm. "Wait till I ring my lawyer."

An elegant gold ring with an enormous diamond in it appeared in his hand. Mr Delmonico looked guilty and tried to hide it behind the bottles of vinegar.

"You can do what you like – you'll have to pay," said the manager.

"*Me? Pay?* Look at my trousers all over jam! I shall lose my temper in a moment. You're just egging me on."

Eggs began to fall out of the air.

A few of them hit the supermarket manager, but most of them broke on Mr Delmonico. He was jam to the knees and egg to the ears.

"Stop it!" cried the manager. "And you talk of lawyers – why, you haven't got a leg to stand on."

Mr Delmonico sat down suddenly in the jam.

"We must get out of this before the balloon goes up," whispered Francis to Sarah, and he found himself rising out of the jam, Sarah beside him. To their delight a beautiful air balloon was carrying them gently away.

"Quick!" said Francis. "Grab Dad."

Catching Mr Delmonico by the collar and by the belt of his trousers his clever twins hoisted

him into the air.

The manager waved his fist at them and shouted: "You haven't heard the last of this."

The balloon swooped through the supermarket door and skimmed over the roofs of the town.

"Home!" ordered Mr Delmonico. "I'm not going to *that* shop again. They have a very funny way of displaying fish and jam."

Francis shook his head. "You shouldn't have teased the word witch, Dad."

"Oh, these word witches need to be teased," Mr Delmonico replied grandly. "Wispy creatures with their heads in the clouds – whereas I am a pretty down-to-earth fellow."

At that moment Mr Delmonico's collar and trouser belt gave way and he fell to earth – fortunately into his very own garden which he had dug and raked that morning until it was as soft as velvet.

"We're home," said Francis, "but the whirling words are still with us. What will we do about that?"

Chef Huey

Ann Cameron

"**F**ood should be different from the way it is," I said to my mum. "Then I wouldn't mind eating it."

"How should it be different?" my mum asked.

"I don't exactly know," I said.

"Maybe you will work it out and be a chef," my mum said.

"What's a chef?" I asked.

"A chef is a very good cook who sometimes invents new things to eat," my mum told me.

The next day we went to the

supermarket. I saw pictures of chefs on some of the food packages. They were all smiling. I wondered if when they were little they had to eat what their parents told them to eat. Maybe that's why they became chefs – so they could invent foods that they liked to eat. Probably that's when they became happy.

The chef with the biggest smile of all was Chef Marco on the tin of Chef Marco's Spaghetti.

"Please get that tin," I said to my mum. "I want to take it home."

I wanted to invent something with it, but I wasn't sure what.

At first I couldn't think of anything it went with. Instead, I thought of cakes like pillows. I thought of carrots that would be fastened together around meat loaf to make skyscrapers on our plates. One night I did tie some carrots around a meat loaf my dad made – but the strings that fastened them came loose in the oven, and the skyscraper fell down.

It was the night before Mother's Day when I thought of a brand new food.

I could see it in my mind. Something yellow. A happy, yellow food. One that didn't mind being eaten.

In the morning, Julian and I were going to bring my mum breakfast in bed. Julian was going to fry eggs. I told him I had a better idea.

"What is it?" he asked.

"Banana spaghetti," I said.

"Banana spaghetti!" he said, "I never heard of it!"

"It's a new invention!" I said. "It will be a one hundred per cent surprise."

Julian likes surprises. "So how do we make it?" he asked.

"Simple!" I said. "We have bananas and we have spaghetti. All we have to do is put them together."

Julian thought about it. "We'd better get up early tomorrow," he said. "Just in case."

At six a.m. we went downstairs very quietly and turned on the lights in the kitchen. We went to work.

We mashed up three ripe bananas. I took out the tin of Chef Marco's Spaghetti. In the picture on the tin, Chef Marco had his arms spread out wide, with a steaming platter balanced above his head on one hand.

I decided to stand that way when I brought Mum the banana spaghetti. I would go up the stairs ahead of Julian with her plate, so Julian couldn't take all the credit.

I held the tin and Julian opened

it. We put the spaghetti in a bowl.
It had a lot of tomato sauce on it –
the colour of blood.

"We have to get the tomato off!"
I said.

We put the spaghetti in the sink
and washed it with hot water. It
got nice and clean. We put it on a
plate.

"It looks kind of spongy," Julian
said.

"It will be good," I said. "We just
need to put the sauce on it."

Julian dumped all the mashed
banana on the top.

"Banana spaghetti!" I said.

"Taste it!" Julian said.

But I wasn't sure I wanted to.

"You try it!" I said.

Julian tasted it. His lips
puckered up. He wiped his mouth

with a kitchen towel.

"It will be better when it's hot," he said.

We put it in a pan on the stove and it got hot. Very hot. The banana scorched. It smelled like burning rubber.

Julian turned off the stove. We looked into the pan.

"Not all of it burned," Julian said. "Just the bottom. We can put the rest on the plates."

"We did. Then we looked at it.

Banana spaghetti was not the way I had imagined it. It wasn't yellow. It was brown. It wasn't happy. It looked miserable.

It looked worse than turnips, worse than aubergine, worse than a baked fish eye.

"Maybe it's better than we

think," Julian said. "When you don't like some stuff, Mum always tells you it's better than you think."

"Will she eat it?" I asked.

"She'll eat it because we made it," Julian said.

"That might not be a good enough reason," I said.

"You can tell her just to try a little bit," Julian advised.

That seemed like a good idea. "Let's take it upstairs," I said. I handed Mums plate to him.

"No," Julian said, "you take it up. It's your invention." He handed the plate back to me.

I put the plate on a tray with a knife and a fork and a napkin. I started up the stairs. I tried holding the tray above my head on

one hand, but it was very tippy. I couldn't do it the way Chef Marco did. And I wasn't happy like Chef Marco, either. I wished Julian was with me.

I climbed five steps. "It's better than you think," I told myself.

On the sixth step I just sat down with the tray in my lap, and stayed there.

145

I heard the door to my parents' room open. I heard feet hurrying down the stairs. My dad's.

He stopped when he saw me.

"Huey," he said, "what are you doing?"

"Thinking," I said. "What are you doing?"

"Going for coffee – what is that stuff you're holding?"

"It's banana spaghetti," I said. "I invented it. Julian and I made it for Mum. We thought it would be good. But it didn't come out the way I wanted it to."

My dad sat by me and looked at it. I passed it to him.

"It does seem to have a problem," he said. "Maybe several problems."

He sniffed it and wrinkled his nose. He got a faraway,

146

professional look on his face, as if he was comparing it with all the banana foods he had ever tasted in his life. He looked as wise as Chef Marco.

"Banana spaghetti," he said. "It's a good idea. You just need to make it differently."

"How!"

"Spaghetti is usually made with flour and eggs," Dad explained. "But I think we could make it from flour and banana. After I have my coffee, we can try."

We went to the kitchen. Julian had the eggs out. He was getting a frying pan.

"You can put that frying pan away, Julian," my dad said. "We're making banana spaghetti."

He flicked the switch on the

coffee maker. In a minute coffee spurted out, and he poured himself a cup and sipped it.

"I'm ready," he said. "Peel me three bananas, boys!"

We did.

"Now put them in this bowl and mash them!" he said.

We did. They came out sort of white, just like the first ones we mashed. And flour wasn't going to change the colour.

"Dad," I said, "I want banana spaghetti to be yellow. It's not going to be yellow, is it?"

"Not without help," my dad said. "Look in the cupboard. Maybe there's some yellow food colouring in there."

We took everything out of the cupboard. Toothpicks, napkins, salt, burn ointment, tins of soup, instant coffee, six pennies, and a spider's web. At the very back I found a tiny bottle of yellow stuff. I showed it to my dad.

"That's it!" he said. "Put some in, Huey! Just a few drops."

I did.

"Stir that yellow around," he said.

We took spoons and did it.

"Bring me the flour," he said.

We did.

He dumped some in the bowl.

"This is hard to mix," my dad said, "so let me do it."

With a fork he mixed the flour and banana into a dough.

"Julian! Spread some flour on this counter!" he said.

Julian did.

My dad set the dough on the floured counter. "I have to knead this dough," he said. "You boys clean the cupboard and put everything back in it."

We did, except for the pennies. We asked if we could have them, and my dad said yes. We put them in our pockets.

Dad rolled up the sleeves of his pyjamas and pushed the dough back and forth under his hands, twisting and turning and pressing it hard, until it was smooth and not sticky.

"The dough has to rest so it will be stretchy," he said. He covered it with an upside-down bowl and put a big pot of water on the stove to boil.

"What should go in the sauce?"

he asked. "It's your invention, Huey, so you decide."

I tried to think of the best ingredient in the world.

"What about . . . whipped cream?" I asked. I never had any spaghetti that way, but I thought it would be good.

"Whipped cream! A great idea!" my dad said.

I poured cream into a bowl. Dad got the electric mixer out, and I beat the cream.

"How about . . . sugar?" Julian said.

"Sugar is right," I said. Julian poured some in.

"Now," Dad said, "what about spices? How about . . . oregano?" And he gave me the oregano bottle so I could smell it.

151

It smelled like pizza. "No!" I said.

"How about . . . cinnamon?" he asked.

Julian and I both smelled the cinnamon. "Yes!" we said.

"And how about . . . ginger?" He handed me the jar.

Julian and I both smelled it. Julian said no. I said yes. Banana spaghetti is mine, so I won. My dad shook in some ginger, and then he beat the cream till it was thick and fluffy.

"How about . . . sliced banana?" Julian said.

I said yes. We sliced a banana. My dad stirred it into the cream.

We all tasted the sauce. It was delicious.

"Now," my dad said, "the spaghetti."

He uncovered the spaghetti dough and asked us for the rolling pin and the flour.

He rolled the dough, and then we rolled it some more. Finally, when it was thin and stretched out like a blanket, he folded it over twice and cut it into strips.

Julian and I separated the strips and unfolded them. They were long and smooth and yellow. We held them in our hands gently, like Christmas-tree tinsel.

The water in the pot was boiling as if it wanted to jump out. We stood on chairs by the stove and dropped in all the spaghetti strings at once. They sank and swam in the pot for just a minute before my dad dipped in a fork and fished one out.

He tasted it.

"Done!" he said. "Quick! Get the plates ready!"

We did. Dad set a strainer in the sink. He poured everything out of the pot. All the water washed down the drain. The spaghetti stayed in the strainer. He divided the spaghetti on the plates and shook some cinnamon over it. I spread the sauce on top. It looked good – except for one thing.

"Just a minute!" I said. I found a bag of chopped peanuts and tossed some on top of each plate of banana spaghetti.

"Is that everything, Huey?" my dad asked.

"Yes," I said.

"Delivery time!" Julian said.

I went first with two plates.

Julian came behind me with the other two plates. My dad came last, with silverware, coffee, and orange juice on a tray.

My hands were full. I knocked on the bedroom door with the edge of one plate.

"Come in!" my mum said. I hoped she would be just waking, but she was sitting up in bed, reading a book. She looked hungry.

I set one plate on the dressing table. I brought the other to her the way Chef Marco would have done it, held out like a gift.

"Happy Mother's Day!" I said.

"What is this?" she said.

"Just . . . banana spaghetti," I said.

My dad handed her a fork. She tasted it.

155

"Delicious!" she said. "Very strange, but very delicious."

"Dad and Julian helped me," I said. "But it's my invention."

We arranged everything so we could all eat on the bed. When we had eaten all the spaghetti, we had second helpings of sauce.

My mum scooped up the last bit of her sauce with a spoon.

"Banana spaghetti! What a wonderful breakfast!" she said.

And I was very proud. Just yesterday there was no such thing as banana spaghetti in the whole world – and now there is. Just like once the telephone didn't exist, or television, or space stations. A lot of people believed those things could never exist. But then some great inventor made them.

I am an inventor. And a chef.

And I know what I want for dinner on my birthday. Banana spaghetti. With chocolate shavings over the sauce, and seven yellow candles on top.

Patrick Comes to School

Margaret Mahy

"**G**raham," said the teacher, "will you look after Patrick at playtime? Remember, he is new to the school and has no friends here yet."

There were lots of things Graham would rather have done, but he had to smile and say, "Yes, Mr Porter."

Behind him Harry Biggs gave his funny, grunting laugh and whispered, "Nursery-nursery

Graham." Mr Porter was watching
so Graham could not say anything
back.

Patrick was a little shrimp of a
boy with red hair – not just
carroty or ginger – a sort of fiery
red. Freckles were all over his
face, crowded like people on a five
o'clock bus, all jostling and
pushing to get the best places. In
fact, Graham thought, Patrick
probably had more freckle than
face. As well as red hair and
freckles, Patrick had a tilted nose
and eyes so blue and bright that he
looked all the time as if he'd just
been given a specially good
Christmas present. He seemed
cheerful, which was something,
but he was a skinny, short little
fellow, not likely to be much good

at sport, or at looking after himself in a fight.

"Just my luck to get stuck with a new boy!" thought Graham.

At playtime he took Patrick round and showed him the football field and the shelter shed. Graham's friend Len came along too. Len and Graham were very polite to Patrick, and he was very polite back, but it wasn't much fun really. Every now and then Len and Graham would look at each other over Patrick's head. It was easy to do, because he was so small. "Gosh, what a nuisance!" the looks said, meaning Patrick.

Just before the bell went, Harry Biggs came up with three other boys. Harry Biggs *was* big, and the three other boys were even bigger, and came from another class.

"Hallo, here's the new boy out with his nurse," said Harry. "What's your name, new boy?"

Graham felt he ought to do something to protect little Patrick, but Patrick spoke out quite boldly and said, "Patrick Fingall O'Donnell." So that was all right.

Harry Biggs frowned at the name. "Now don't be too smart!" he said. "We tear cheeky little kids apart in this school, don't we?" He nudged the other boys, who grinned and shuffled. "Where do you live, O'Donnell?"

Then Patrick said a funny thing. "I live in a house among the trees, and we've got a golden bird sitting on our gate."

He didn't sound as if he was

joking. He spoke carefully as if he was asking Harry Biggs a difficult riddle. He sounded as if, in a minute, he might be laughing at Harry Biggs. Harry Biggs must have thought so too, because he frowned even harder and said, "Remember what I told you, and don't be too clever. Now listen . . . what does your father do?"

"Cut it out, Harry," said Graham quickly. "Pick on someone your own size."

"I'm not hurting him, Nursey!" exclaimed Harry. "Go on, Ginger, what does he do for a crust?"

Patrick answered quickly, almost as if he was reciting a poem.

"My father wears clothes with gold all over them," said Patrick. "In the morning he says to the men,

'I'll have a look at my elephants this morning,' and he goes and looks at his elephants. When he says the word, the elephants kneel down. He can ride the elephants all day if he wants to, but mostly he is too busy with the lions or his monkeys or his bears."

Harry Biggs stared at Patrick with his eyes popping out of his head.

"Who do you think you're kidding?" he said at last. "Are you making out your dad's a king or something? Nobody wears clothes with gold on them."

"My father does!" said Patrick. "Wears them every day!" He thought for a moment. "All these lions and tigers lick his hands," he added.

"Does he work in a circus?" asked one of the other boys.

"No!" said Patrick. "We'd live in a caravan then, not a house with a golden bird at the gate." Once again Graham felt that Patrick was turning his answers into riddles.

Before anyone could say any more the bell rang to go back into school.

"Gee, you'll hear all about that!" Len said to Patrick. "Why did you tell him all that stuff?"

"It's true," Patrick said. "He asked me, and it's true."

"He'll think you were taking the mickey," Graham said. "Anyway, it couldn't be true."

"It *is* true," said Patrick, "and it isn't taking the mickey to say what's true, is it?"

"Well, I don't know," Graham muttered to Len. "It doesn't sound very true to me."

Of course Harry Biggs and the other boys spread the story round the school.

Children came up to Patrick and said, "Hey, does your father wear pure gold?"

"Not all gold," said Patrick. "Just quite a lot."

Then the children would laugh and pretend to faint with laughing.

"Hey, Ginger!" called Harry Biggs. "How's all the elephants?"

"All right, thank you," Patrick would reply politely. Once he added, "We've got a monkey too, at present, and he looks just like you." But he only said it once, because Harry Biggs pulled his hair and twisted his ears. Patrick's ears were nearly as red as his hair.

"Serves you right for showing off," said Graham.

"Well, I might have been showing off a bit," Patrick admitted. "It's hard not to sometimes."

Yet, although they teased him, slowly children came to like

Patrick. Graham liked him a lot.
He was so good-tempered and full
of jokes. Even when someone was
laughing at him, he laughed too.
The only thing that worried
Graham was the feeling that
Patrick was laughing at some
secret joke, or at any rate at some
quite different thing.

"Don't you get sick of being
teased?" he asked.

"Well, I'm a bit sick of it now,"
Patrick said, "but mostly I don't
mind. Anyhow, what I said was
true, and that's all there is to say."

"I'd hate to be teased so much,"
Graham said. But he could see
Patrick was like a rubber ball – the
harder you knocked him down, the
faster and higher he bounced
back.

The wonderful day came when
the class was taken to the zoo.
Even Harry Biggs, who usually
made fun of school outings, looked
forward to this one.

Off they went in the school bus,
and Mr Porter took them round.

". . . like the Pied Piper of
Hamelin," said Patrick, "with all
the rats following him."

"Who are you calling a rat,
Ginger?" said Harry Biggs sourly.

Everywhere at the zoo was the
smell of animals, birds and straw.
They had a map which showed
them the quickest way to go round
the zoo, and the first lot of cages
they went past held birds. There
were all sizes and colours of birds
from vultures to canaries. One
cage held several bright parrots.

The parrots watched the children pass with round, wise eyes. Then suddenly the biggest and gayest of the lot flew from his perch and clung to the wire, peering out at them.

"Patrick! Hallo, Patrick dear!" it said. "Hallo! Hallo! Hallo, Patrick! Hallo, dear!"

Mr Porter looked at Patrick.

"Oh yes," he said. "I forgot about you, Patrick. It's a bit of a busman's holiday for you, isn't it?"

As the walked away the parrot went on screaming after them, "Hallo, Patrick! Patrick! Hallo, dear!" in its funny parrot voice.

On they went past the lions and tigers. Len and Graham stole sideways glances at Patrick, and so did Harry Biggs and several other children. Patrick looked as wide-eyed and interested as anyone else. He did not seem to see the glances at all.

They went past the bearpits, and then up a hill where there was nothing but trees. Among the trees, beside a stone fence, was a little house. On one of the gateposts was a brass peacock, polished until it shone, and below that was a little notice saying "Head Keeper's Cottage".

Now, for the first time, Patrick suddenly turned and grinned at Graham.

"*That's* where I live," he whispered.

They were all looking into the bearpits ten minutes later when a man came hurrying to meet them.

He was wearing a lot of gold braid all over his blue uniform. There was gold braid round his cap and his brass buttons shone like little suns. His eyes were blue and bright and his face was covered with freckles – more freckle than face you might have said. He stopped to speak to Mr Porter and took off his cap.

His hair was as red as fire.

"Is *that* your father?" Graham asked.

"Yes," said Patrick. "See, I told you he wore a lot of gold."

"Huh!" said Harry Biggs. "Well, why didn't you say when I asked you . . . why didn't you say he was a keeper at the zoo?"

"Head Keeper!" said Graham, feeling suddenly very proud of Patrick.

"Ordinary keepers don't have gold," Patrick pointed out.

"Why didn't you say?" Harry repeated. "Trying to be clever, eh?"

"I don't like things to sound too ordinary," said Patrick, sounding rather self-satisfied. "I like them to be noble and sort of mysterious."

172

"Well, you're mad," said Harry, but no one was taking any notice of him. Mr Porter and Mr O'Donnell, Head Keeper, came back to them.

"This is Mr O'Donnell," said Mr Porter. "He has offered to let us have a look at the young lion cubs. They aren't on view to the public yet, so we are very lucky. And don't worry – the mother lion won't be there, so none of you will get eaten."

As they went on their way a foolish little girl said to Patrick, "Have you got any other relatives who do interesting things, Patrick?"

"Shut up!" said Graham, but it was too late.

"My uncle," said Patrick without

any hesitation. "He's my great-uncle really, though. He eats razor blades for a living, razor blades and burning matches."

"No one can eat razor blades!" shouted Harry Biggs.

"Well, my great-uncle does," said Patrick, and this time everyone believed him.

PS Patrick's great-uncle was a magician.

The Day Michael Made the News

Philippa Werry

Once there was a boy called
Michael, whose family only
liked watching TV. They watched
TV at breakfast, and after school,
and during dinner, and before bed.

Michael liked going to the park
to play football or cricket, but his
dad only liked sport on TV.

Michael liked going to the zoo to
look at the animals, but his mum
only liked nature programmes on
TV.

Michael liked playing games and making models, but his brother and sister only liked game shows on TV.

One day, Michael was walking home after playing football when he heard a lot of shouting coming from the dairy.

There was a bang, and another bang, and a scream, and a crash.

A man with a mask over his face, and a bag in his hand, rushed out of the dairy and jumped into a car. The car sped off, nearly knocking over two old men and a boy on a bike.

Michael's eyes were nearly popping out of his head, but he wrote down the car's number plate on the back of his hand.

Lots of people came out of the

other shops, and next minute the
police arrived, and the TV crews.

When the police asked if anyone
had noticed the number on the
number plate, everyone shook
their heads. Then Michael stepped
forward shyly, and told them that
he had written it down.

The police were very pleased.
"Well done!" they said, and they

took him for a ride in the police car to the police station, and then they took him home.

Michael hoped his family would see him drive up in a real police car, but everyone was inside watching TV.

"Mum! Dad! Everyone!" he shouted as he came in the front door. "Guess what happened! Guess where I've been!"

"Hush! Shush!" they all said. "We're watching the news!"

"*I've* got some news," said Michael. "I was just walking home, and—"

"Look at that!" exclaimed his dad, still watching the TV screen. "Someone tried to rob the dairy down the road!"

"That's what I'm telling you,"

Michael said. "I was walking past, and—"

"They fired two shots!" his mum called out. "Just fancy that!"

"I *heard* them," Michael said. "Then the man came running out—"

"The robber ran out and got into a waiting car," said his sister. "Quiet, Michael, I want to hear what happened next."

"I'll tell you," said Michael. "The car drove off, and—"

"Someone wrote down the car's number," said Michael's brother. "That was quick thinking."

"It was *me*," Michael shouted. "*I* wrote it down. Look, there I am on TV!"

Sure enough, there was his face filling up the whole screen, and his voice telling the TV reporter what had happened.

"That boy looks just like Michael!" cried his mother, and his father, and his sister and brother.

They all turned round to look at him.

"Where *have* you been, Michael?" asked his mother. "You're very late home."

"I'll tell you," said Michael, "If you'll only *listen*."

And, for once, they did.

Melanie Brown is Too Helpful

Pamela Oldfield

The school television set was not at all like the set in Melanie Brown's home. It was much bigger and stood on four legs, at one end of the hall. There were two doors at the front which were always kept locked until the teachers opened them with a small key. When it was time to watch the television the children all carried chairs into the hall and arranged them in rows.

Melanie Brown looked forward to the television programmes. One was about puppets and the other was about fire engines and shops and animals and aeroplanes – and so many things there is no time to tell them all! As soon as they went into the hall Miss Bradley would switch the set on at the wall, and while it was warming up she would pull the curtains to shut out the light.

Now one day Melanie Brown was feeling helpful. She had given out the milk without spilling a single drop. She had found a missing piece of jigsaw, and she had cleaned the blackboard. She was still feeling particularly helpful when they went into the hall to watch the puppets. To her surprise

Miss Bradley went straight over to the windows to pull the curtains, so Melanie Brown guessed at once that she had forgotten to switch the set on and without a moment's hesitation she ran across to the wall and flicked the switch! She was very pleased with herself. Four helpful things in one morning! She sat down on her chair feeling very proud and they all waited for the programme to begin.

They waited and waited – and waited! But nothing happened.

"That's funny," said Miss Bradley. "I wonder what's wrong. It was working before playtime. I'll have a look at it."

She looked at the back of the set to see if the aerial was properly connected, because sometimes it worked loose. Not this time, though. She twiddled all the knobs and tried the other channels. Nothing. She looked up at the clock and frowned.

"Oh dear! We have missed the beginning," she said. "I had better tell Miss Grainger. Just sit quietly for a moment, children."

Miss Grainger was the headmistress, so they all knew it was a serious matter. They sat like mice until Miss Bradley and Miss Grainger came into the hall. Miss Grainger did all the things that Miss Bradley had done but still the television remained quite blank.

"How very odd," said Miss Grainger. "You say it was working perfectly before play?"

"Yes," said Miss Bradley. "Mrs Jones's class watched something and she left it on for us."

"I'll give Mr Bloggs a ring," said Miss Grainger. "It will only take a minute or two to have a look at it. And what nice patient children you are!" she said, turning to them. "I think Melanie Brown is one of the quietest."

Melanie Brown beamed with delight and Miss Bradley smiled at her. Soon Mr Bloggs arrived on his bicycle with a book of instructions in his pocket. He marched into the hall and opened the book importantly. Then he glared at Miss Bradley.

"Can't we have a bit more light in here?" he asked sternly, and Miss Bradley hurried to draw back the curtains. He turned over several pages and said "Aha!" and scratched his nose. Melanie Brown thought it was almost as much fun watching Mr Bloggs as it would have been watching the puppets!

"I think it's your power pack," he said at last and retired behind the set. They could see his feet and legs and they could hear him breathing heavily. Then he said

"Damn!" in a loud voice.

Melanie Brown was shocked.

"He said 'Damn'," she said. "He shouldn't say that!"

"Poor Mr Bloggs," said Miss Bradley. "I'm sure he didn't mean it. I think he's hurt himself."

Mr Bloggs reappeared, looking hot and flustered.

"Can't have been off long," he grumbled. "It's still hot!"

He looked hopefully at the screen, which remained empty.

"Why don't you thump it?" cried Christopher. "That's what my dad does!"

Mr Bloggs raised his hand and for one thrilling moment they thought he was going to, but he hesitated.

"Better not," he said reluctantly,

dropping his hand. He had another look in his book, then shook his head.

"Could it be something wrong with the aerial itself?" suggested Miss Bradley.

"Ah, that'll be it!" he said. "I reckon you've hit the nail on the head! The aerial! Now that'll be a job for the aerial people, not me! I'll tell Miss Grainger to get in touch with them right away."

They watched him go regretfully.

"Now we can't see the puppets," wailed Denise.

"Never mind," said Miss Bradley. "I expect it will be minded in time for tomorrow's programme. Now, take your chairs back to the class-room. I'll just switch off the—"

She stopped in the middle of the

sentence and stared at the switch. "It's not switched on! But Mrs Jones said it was!"

She put the switch down and waited, watching the set. Music and pictures appeared and all the children clapped their hands and cheered. But Miss Bradley didn't cheer. She switched it off again and looked round. The children took one look at her face and stopped cheering.

"Did anyone touch this switch?" she asked quietly.

Melanie Brown put her hand up and Miss Bradley groaned.

"Not you again, Melanie?" she said faintly.

"I only switched it on," said Melanie Brown, "because you forgot."

"I did *not* forget!" said Miss
Bradley. "I didn't need to switch it
on because it was already on! You
must have switched it off!"

There was a terrible silence.

"Oh well, I suppose you didn't
mean it," said Miss Bradley. "But I
don't think Miss Grainger's going
to be too pleased about it."

Melanie Brown though it was
very ungrateful of Miss Bradley to
talk like that and decided not to
help her ever again. She told Miss
Bradley what she had decided and
Miss Bradley said, "Is that a
threat or a promise!"

Sometimes, thought Melanie
Brown, teachers could be very
difficult!

Vardiello

Retold by Geoffrey Summerfield

There was once a very sensible woman who lived with her only son. His name was Vardiello, and he was a real fool.

One day, the mother had to run an errand, so she said to her silly lad: "Now, listen. I've got to go out for an hour or two. The old hen in the shed is sitting on a dozen eggs, and they should be hatching out soon. So you must make sure she stays on the eggs and keeps them warm. If she wanders off to go scratching about in the yard, just

look sharp and see that she gets
back to the nest, double quick. Or
we shall have no chickens. You
understand?"

"Don't you worry about a thing.
I'll take care of everything."

"And one more thing. That new
pot in the cupboard. If you so
much as nibble what's in that pot,
you'll be dead before you can say
Jack Robinson. So leave well
alone."

"Thanks for the warning. I'll go
nowhere near it."

Now, as soon as his mother had
gone, Vardiello went into the
garden, and he dug holes all over,
and covered them with twigs and
clods, to try to catch the lads that
used to come scrumping in the
apple trees. He worked hard for an

hour or more, and he was just
rubbing his aching back when he
saw the old hen come waddling
into the garden for a good scratch
around.

"Back you go! Shoo! Shoo! Hish!
Hish! Back to your eggs! Go on!"

But the hen just ignored him. So
he stamped his feet. Then he threw
his cap at her. But it made no
difference. The old hen just went
on with her scratching. So
Vardiello got into a real panic, and
he picked up a big stick and threw
it at her!

Bonk! It hit the poor old hen
right on the head, and there she
lay, in the dust, dead as a doornail.

"Oh, the eggs! The chickens!"
Vardiello cried. And he rushed
into the shed. He put his hand on

the eggs and they were almost
stone-cold. So he sat on them, to
warm them up again, and his
trousers were plastered with
smashed eggs. What a mess! he
tried to scrape it all off, but his
hands were just smeared with goo,
so he wriggled out of his trousers
and washed them in the kitchen
sink. He didn't have time to dry
them, and they were his only pair,
so he put them on again while they
were still sopping wet, and his legs
felt clammy from top to bottom.

By this time, he was so hungry
that his stomach was rumbling
like thunder. So he went out and
found the poor old hen. He
plucked her and cleaned her, lit a
fire in the grate, and cooked her.

When the old hen was well

cooked, he put her just outside the
kitchen door to cool off. Then he
decided to do himself proud, and
spread a clean cloth on the table.
Then he went down to the cellar
with a large jug to get some wine
to drink with his meal: in those
days, people didn't drink tea, but
used to keep a great barrel of wine
in the cellar, to drink with their
meals.

So he put his jug under the tap of the barrel, and turned the tap on. He was watching all the bubbles sparkling in the jug, when he heard a terrible clattering and banging upstairs. So he rushed out of the cellar, and there were two great tom-cats fighting over his chicken.

He chased those cats all over the yard, and they dashed into the house to hide. So he chased them all over the house, upstairs and downstairs, until the cats dropped the old hen under the bed. By the time he'd picked it up and cleaned it, he suddenly remembered the wine-tap: it was still running!

So he dashed down to the cellar, and the barrel was empty. The wine was all over the floor, a great flood. Now he had to work out a plan to prevent his mother from finding out. He took a sack of flour, and scattered it all over the cellar floor, to soak up all the wine.

Then he sat down, and thought. "No fat hen! No eggs! No chickens! No wine! No flour! No hope!"

He didn't dare face his mother when she came back, so he decided to do away with himself. He remembered what she had said about the new pot in the cupboard. She'd said he would die if he even nibbled whatever was in that pot. So he rushed up out of the cellar, slipping and sliding on the flour paste on the floor, and rushed to the cupboard. He snatched the pot off the shelf and gulped down everything, glug, glug, munch, munch, until the pot was empty.

Then he went and hid in the oven, and waited to die.

When his mother got back, she knocked and knocked. She had always told him to lock the door when she went out, so she waited for him to come and open it. She knocked and knocked, then she knocked again until her knuckles were sore. Then she lost her patience and kicked the door open.

"Vardiello! Vardiello! Where are you? What are you up to? Are you deaf? Come out, come out, wherever you are! Do you hear?"

And a thin squeaky voice came out of the oven: "I'm in here. In the oven. But you'll never see me again. I shall be dead in a minute!"

"Don't talk daft!"

"But I shall. I've eaten the poison in the pot. And I'm dying."

Then his mother sat down and laughed until she cried. The tears poured down her face, and her handkerchief was soaking wet.

"Tell me all about it," she said, when she could speak. "You silly billy! Tell me what happened."

So he told her all about the old hen, the eggs, the cats, the wine, the flour, and the poison in the pot.

"Oh, the pot!" his mother said. "It was full of pickled walnuts. I was saving them for a rainy day. I just didn't want you to eat them. So I warned you to leave well alone! But they weren't poison.

You'll just have a stomach-ache. Now come out of that oven and stretch your legs."

So Vardiello clambered out of the oven. And he felt very foolish. Then his mother gave him a glass of milk.

"Now, what are we going to do for food?" she asked him. "No eggs. No chickens. No hen. No flour. No wine. Dear me, I shall have to sell that cloth I've been weaving."

So she went up to her bedroom and came down with her arms full of a great roll of fine cloth.

"Take this into the market and sell it," she told Vardiello. "But be careful. People who talk a lot, and use big words, are probably trying to cheat you. So be on your guard."

"Don't you worry about a thing,"Vardiello told his mother, and carried the cloth off to market.

"Cloth! Fine cloth!" he shouted. But whenever anybody said, "I'd like to buy some of your cloth," he remembered what his mother had said. *They talk too much*, he thought, so he didn't sell even a square inch, for fear of being cheated. "Cloth! Cloth!" he shouted, over and over again, for hours on end, until he was worn out. Then he wandered off, out of the market place, until he came to a statue. His feet were so sore by this time, that he sat on the ground to rest, and leaned against the statue.

"A customer!" he thought,

looking at the statue. "He could do with some cloth to make some new clothes."

"Would you like to buy some cloth?" he asked the statue. No reply.

"It's very good. Don't you like the look of it?" No reply.

"This is the man for me," Vardiello whispered.

"It will suit you, sir," he said to the statue. "I'll leave it with you. Then you can have a good look at it. You can pay me tomorrow. I'll come back then."

Then he rushed home to tell his mother all about his success.

"Oh, you idiot! You can't be trusted to do anything! What am I going to do with you?"

"But, but, Mother, wait till

tomorrow. You'll see. I'll get the
money for your cloth. Just wait
and see."

The next day, Vardiello rushed
off to collect his money from the
statue. He had left the cloth by the
feet of the statue and, of course,
the first person to pass that way
had walked off with it.

"I've come for my money. The
money for the cloth I left with you
yesterday."

The statue said nothing.

"My money!" Vardiello shouted.
"Money for the cloth."

The statue said not a word.

"My money!" Vardiello shouted.
He was almost weeping with anger
by this time, and he rushed to pick
up a brick and hurled it at the
statue.

And lo and behold, the statue
smashed to smithereens! And
inside the broken statue, Vardiello
found a pot full of gold coins.

Vardiello snatched it up, and
laughed out loud. Then he ran all
the way home.

"Mother! Mother! Payment!
Money for the cloth!"

When his mother saw the pot full

of gold coins she was amazed. Then she thought, *Vardiello is going to tell everybody about this gold. I must do something, quick!*

"Thank you, son. Put it all in the cupboard. Then go to the front door and wait for the milkman. I don't want to miss him."

So Vardiello went and sat just outside the front door. And his mother went upstairs, opened the bedroom window, and dropped a shower of nuts and raisins, currants, figs and dates on the lad. Vardiello couldn't believe his eyes. He caught them in his hands in his mouth, then he called out to his mother.

"Mother! Mother! It's raining figs, and dates, and nuts, and raisins! Bring a bowl! Quick!"

So his mother slipped downstairs very quietly on tiptoe and collected her nuts and dates and the currants and raisins in a bowl. And she let Vardiello eat till he was fit to burst and fell asleep.

A few weeks later, two men were arguing in the street. One of them had found a gold coin in his back garden, and his neighbour was trying to claim it for his own. Vardiello heard them and said, "Ridiculous! Arguing about a single gold coin! I found a whole potful of them!"

So the men dragged him off to the police station, and the chief of police said to Vardiello, "Now, my young man, tell me all about your pot of gold."

"It's very simple, sir. I found it a few weeks ago inside a dumb man who stole a roll of my mother's cloth, on the day it rained figs, and raisins, and currants, and nuts, and . . ."

"A fine tail our cat's got," said the chief of police. "Now, run along, my lad, and don't let your imagination run away with you!"

And Vardiello and his mother lived happily ever after. Whenever they needed food, they took a coin out of the pot in their cupboard, and nobody ever believed a word of Vardiello's story.

Perfect Peter's Horrid Day

Francesca Simon

"Henry, use your fork!" said Dad.

"*I'm* using my fork," said Peter.

"Henry, sit down!" said Mum.

"*I'm* sitting down," said Peter.

"Henry, stop spitting!" said Dad.

"*I'm* not spitting," said Peter.

"Henry, chew with your mouth shut!" said Mum.

"*I'm* chewing with my mouth shut," said Peter.

"Henry, don't make a mess!" said Dad.

"*I'm* not making a mess," said Peter.

"What?" said Mum.

Perfect Peter was not having a perfect day.

Mum and Dad are too busy yelling at Henry all the time to notice how good I *am*, thought Peter.

When was the last time Mum and Dad had said, "Marvellous, Peter, you're using your fork!" "Wonderful, Peter, you're sitting down!" "Superb, Peter, you're not spitting!" "Fabulous, Peter, you're chewing with your mouth shut!" "Perfect, Peter, you never make a mess!"

Perfect Peter dragged himself upstairs.

Everyone just expects me to be perfect, thought Peter, as he wrote his Aunt Agnes a thank-you note for the super thermal vests. *It's not fair*.

From downstairs came the sound of raised voices.

"Henry, get your muddy shoes off the sofa!" yelled Dad.

"Henry, stop being so horrid!" yelled Mum.

Then Perfect Peter started to think.

What if I *were horrid?* thought Peter.

Peter's mouth dropped open. What a horrid thought! He looked around quickly to see if anyone had noticed.

He was alone in his immaculate bedroom. No one would ever know he'd thought such a terrible thing.

But imagine being horrid. No, that would never do.

Peter finished his letter, read a few pages of his favourite magazine *Best Boy*, got into bed and turned off his light without being asked.

Imagine being horrid.

What if *I were horrid*, thought Peter. I *wonder what would happen?*

When Peter woke up the next morning, he did not dash downstairs to get breakfast ready. Instead, he lazed in bed for an extra five minutes.

When he finally got out of bed, Peter did not straighten the duvet.

Nor did Peter plump his pillows.

Instead, Peter looked at his tidy bedroom and had a very wicked thought.

Quickly, before he could change his mind, he took off his pyjama top and did not fold it neatly. Instead he dropped it on the floor.

Mum came in.

"Good morning, darling. You must be tired, sleeping in."

Peter hoped Mum would notice his untidy room.

But Mum did not say anything.

"Notice anything, Mum?" said Peter.

Mum looked around.

"No," said Mum.

"Oh," said Peter.

"What?" said Mum.

"I haven't made my bed," said Peter.

"Clever you to remember it's washday," said Mum. She stripped the sheets and duvet cover, then swooped and picked up Peter's pyjama top.

"Thank you, dear," said Mum. She smiled and left.

Peter frowned. Clearly, he would need to work harder at being horrid.

He looked at his beautifully arranged books.

"No!" he gasped, as a dreadful thought sneaked into his head.

Then Peter squared his shoulders. Today was his horrid day, and horrid he would be. He went up to his books and knocked them over.

"*Henry!*" bellowed Dad. "Get up this minute!"

Henry slumped past Peter's door.

Peter decided he would call Henry a horrid name.

"Hello, Ugly," said Peter. Then he went wild and stuck out his tongue.

Henry marched into Peter's bedroom. He glared at Peter.

"What did you call me?" said Henry.

Peter screamed.

Mum ran into the room.

"Stop being horrid, Henry! Look what a mess you've made in here!"

"He called me Ugly," said Henry.

"Of course he didn't," said Mum.

"He did too," said Henry.

"Peter never calls people names," said Mum. "Now pick up those books you knocked over."

"I didn't knock them over," said Henry.

"Well, who did, then, the man in the moon?" said Mum.

Henry pointed at Peter.

"He did," said Henry.

"*Did* you, Peter?" asked Mum.

Peter wanted to be really, really horrid and tell a lie. But he couldn't.

"I did it, Mum," said Peter. Boy, would he get told off now.

"Don't be silly, of course you didn't," said Mum. "You're just saying that to protect Henry."

Mum smiled at Peter and frowned at Henry.

"Now leave Peter alone and get dressed," said Mum.

"But it's the weekend," said Henry.

215

"So?" said Mum.

"But Peter's not dressed."

"I'm sure he was just about to get dressed before you barged in," said Mum. "See? He's already taken his pyjama top off."

"I don't want to get dressed," said Peter boldly.

"You poor boy," said Mum. "You must be feeling ill. Pop back into bed and I'll bring your breakfast up. Just let me put some clean sheets on."

Perfect Peter scowled a tiny scowl. Clearly, he wasn't very good at being horrid yet. He would have to try harder.

At lunch Peter ate pasta with his fingers. No one noticed.

Then Henry scooped up pasta

with both fists and slurped some into his mouth.

"Henry! Use your fork!" said Dad.

Peter spat into his plate.

"Peter, are you choking?" said Dad.

Henry spat across the table.

"Henry! Stop that disgusting spitting this instant!" said Mum.

Peter chewed with his mouth open.

"Peter, is there something wrong with your teeth?" asked Mum.

Henry chomped and dribbled and gulped with his mouth as wide open as possible.

"Henry! This is your last warning. Keep your mouth shut when you eat!" shouted Dad.

Peter did not understand. Why didn't anyone notice how horrid he was? He stretched out his foot and kicked Henry under the table.

Henry kicked him back harder.

Peter shrieked.

Henry got told off. Peter got dessert.

Perfect Peter did not know what to do. No matter how hard he tried to be horrid, nothing seemed to work.

"Now boys," said Mum,

"Grandma is coming for tea this afternoon. Please keep the house tidy and leave the chocolates alone."

"What chocolates?" said Henry.

"Never you mind," said Mum. "You'll have some when Grandma gets here."

Then Peter had a truly stupendously horrid idea. He left the table without waiting to be excused and sneaked into the sitting room.

Peter searched high. Peter searched low. Then Peter found a large box of chocolates hidden behind some books.

Peter opened the box. Then he took a tiny bite out of every single chocolate. When he found good ones with gooey chocolate fudge centres he ate them. The yucky raspberry and strawberry and lemon creams he put back.

Hee Hee, thought Peter. He felt excited. What he had done was absolutely awful. Mum and Dad were sure to notice.

Then Peter looked round the tidy sitting room. Why not mess it up a bit?

Peter grabbed a cushion from the sofa. He was just about to fling it on the floor when he heard someone sneaking into the room.

"What are you doing?" said Henry.

"Nothing, Ugly," said Peter.

"Don't call me Ugly, Toad," said Henry.

"Don't call me Toad, Ugly," said Peter.

"Toad!"

"Ugly!"

"*Toad!*"

"*Ugly!*"

Mum and Dad ran in.

"Henry!" shouted Dad. "Stop being horrid!"

"I'm not being horrid!" said Henry. "Peter is calling me names."

Mum and Dad looked at each other. What was going on?

"Don't lie, Henry," said Mum.

"I did call him a name, Mum," said Peter. "I called him Ugly because he is ugly. So there."

Mum stared at Peter.

Dad stared at Peter.

Henry stared at Peter.

"If Peter did call you a name, it's because you called him one first," said Mum. "Now leave Peter alone."

Mum and Dad left.

"Serves you right, Henry," said Peter.

"You're very strange today," said Henry.

"No I'm not," said Peter.

"Oh yes you are," said Henry. "You can't fool me. Listen, want to play a trick on Grandma?"

"No!" said Peter.

Ding dong.

"Grandma's here!" called Dad.

Mum, Dad, Henry, Peter and Grandma sat down together in the sitting room.

"Let me take your bag, Grandma," said Henry sweetly.

"Thank you dear," said Grandma.

When no one was looking Henry took Grandma's glasses out of her bag and hid them behind Peter's cushion.

Mum and Dad passed around tea and home-made biscuits on the best china plates.

Peter sat on the edge of the sofa and held his breath. Any second now Mum would get out the box of half-eaten chocolates.

Mum stood up and got the box.

"Peter, would you like to pass round the chocolates?" said Mum.

"OK," said Peter. His knees felt wobbly. Everyone was about to find out what a horrid thing he had done.

Peter held out the box.

"Would you like a chocolate,

Mum?" said Peter. His heart
pounded.

"No thanks," said Mum.

"What about me?" said Henry.

"Would you like a chocolate,
Dad?" said Peter. His hands shook.

"No thanks," said Dad.

"What about me!" said Henry.

"Shh, Henry," said Mum. "Don't
be so rude."

"Would you like a chocolate,
Grandma?" said Peter.

There was no escape now.
Grandma loved chocolates.

"Yes, please!" said Grandma. She
peered closely into the box. "Let
me see, what shall I choose? Now,
where are my specs?"

Grandma reached into her bag
and fumbled about.

"That's funny," said Grandma. "I

was sure I'd brought them. Never mind."

Grandma reached into the box, chose a chocolate and popped it into her mouth.

"Oh," said Grandma. "Strawberry cream. Go on, Peter have a chocolate."

"No thanks," said Peter.

"*What about me!*" screamed Horrid Henry.

"None for you," said Dad. "That's not how you ask."

Peter gritted his teeth. If no one was going to notice the chewed chocolates he'd have to do it himself.

"I will have a chocolate," announced Peter loudly. "Hey! Who's eaten all the fudge ones? And who's taken bites out of the rest?"

"Henry!" yelled Mum. "I've told you a million times to leave the chocolates alone!"

"It wasn't me!" said Henry. "It was Peter!"

"Stop blaming Peter," said Dad. "You know he never eats sweets."

"It's not fair!" shrieked Henry. Then he snatched the box from Peter. "I want some *Chocolates!*"

Peter snatched it back. The open box fell to the floor. Chocolates flew everywhere.

"*Henry, go to your room!*" yelled Mum.

"*It's not fair!*" screeched Henry. "I'll get you for this, Peter!"

Then Horrid Henry ran out of the room, slamming the door behind him.

Grandma patted the sofa beside

her. Peter sat down. He could not believe it. What did a boy have to do to get noticed?

"How's my best boy?" asked Grandma.

Peter sighed.

Grandma gave him a big hug. "You're the best boy in the world, Peter, did you know that?"

Peter glowed. Grandma was

right! He was the best.

But wait. Today he was horrid.

No! He was perfect. His horrid day was over.

He was much happier being perfect, anyway. Being horrid was horrible.

I've had my horrid day, thought Peter. *Now I can be perfect again.*

What a marvellous idea. Peter smiled and leaned back against the cushion.

Crunch!

"Oh dear," said Grandma. "That sounds like my specs. I wonder how they got there."

Mum looked at Peter.

Dad looked at Peter.

"It wasn't me!" said Peter.

"Of course not," said Grandma.

"I must have dropped them. Silly me."

"Hmmmn," said Dad.

Perfect Peter ran into the kitchen and looked about. *Now that I'm perfect again, what good deeds can I do?* he thought.

Then Peter noticed all the dirty teacups and plates piled up on the worktop. He had never done the washing up all by himself before Mum and Dad would be so pleased.

Peter carefully washed and dried all the dishes.

Then he stacked them up and carried them to the cupboard.

"*Booooooo!*" shrieked Horrid Henry, leaping out from behind the door.

Crash!

Henry vanished.

Mum and Dad ran in.

The best china lay in pieces all over the floor.

"*Peter!!!*" yelled Mum and Dad.

"*You horrid boy!*" yelled Mum.

"*Go to your room!*" yelled Dad.

"But . . . but . . ." gasped Peter.

"*No buts!*" shouted Mum. "*Go!* Oh, my lovely dishes!"

Perfect Peter ran to his room.

"*Ahhhhhhhhhhh!*" shrieked Peter.

Lazy Jack

Andrew Matthews

Jack lived with his widowed mother. Jack's mother took in washing and ironing and worked hard to earn a bit of money, but Jack didn't do any work at all. He was so lazy, he wouldn't even feed himself. When they had peas, his mother would use a spoon to flick them across the room into Jack's mouth.

One Monday, Jack's mother could stand it no more. She told Jack that if he didn't start earning his keep, she'd turn him out of the house. So on Tuesday, Jack got himself a day's work at Palm Farm, and the farmer, Mr Palmer, paid him a penny. Because he'd never earned wages before, Jack didn't know what to do with the penny. He held it tightly in his hand, but it slipped out of his grip and lost itself as he was crossing a stream on his way home.

"You silly boy!" his mother told him. "You should have put it in your pocket!"

"You know best, Mother," said Jack.

On Wednesday, Jack went to work for Howard the Cowherd, who gave him a big jug of milk for his wages. Jack put the jug in his pocket, but by the time he got home all the milk had sloshed out

of it and he was wetter than a
fish's slippers.

"You silly boy!" said his mother.
"You should have carried it home
on your head!"

"I won't be so silly next time,"
said Jack.

Thursday came, and Jack got a
job at Mary's Dairy. Mary paid
him with a big slab of butter. Jack
put the butter on his head and off
he went. It was such a hot day that
by the time he reached home, the
butter had melted into his hair
and made it as greasy as the inside
of an old frying pan.

"You silly boy!" said his mother.
"You should have carried it home
in your hands!"

"I won't make that mistake
again," said Jack.

On Friday, Jack worked for Mr
Laker the Baker, who gave him a
handsome tom-cat. Jack carried
the cat in his hands, but the cat
wriggled so much it was like
carrying a furry python. Before
he'd gone very far, old Tom gave
him such a bite with his sharp
teeth and such a scratch with his
sharp claws that Jack let him go.

"You silly boy!" said his mother.

"You should have tied a rope around it and walked it home!"

"Of course I should! You're quite right," said Jack.

On Saturday, Jack went to work for Mr Mopp at the butcher's shop. Mr Mopp was so pleased with him that he gave him a string of sausages for his pay. Jack tied a rope around the sausages and walked them home. By the time he got there, the sausages were covered in so much grit and dust that they had to be thrown away.

"You silly boy!" said his mother. "You should have carried them home over your shoulders!"

"Whatever you say, Mother," said Jack.

The following Monday, Jack went to work for Mr Howman the

Ploughman, and Mr Howman gave him a donkey. The donkey kicked and brayed, but at last Jack got it over his shoulders and staggered home.

On the way, Jack met a couple of strangers – a farmer and his little daughter. The daughter had been ill and since her illness she'd been as miserable as rain in a rusty tin. The farmer had taken his daughter to the best doctors in the land, and they'd all told him the only thing that would make her properly better was to have a good laugh. The farmer had heard about how silly the people of Waffam were and he was bringing her on a visit in the hope that something would make her chuckle.

Well, when she saw Jack stumbling along the road with a donkey over his shoulders, and the donkey's ears and legs waggling about in the air, the girl laughed until tears filled her eyes and she was better at once.

The farmer was so overjoyed, he gave Jack a big bag of gold.

"You ride home on the donkey, lad, and keep a tight hold on that bag of money," said the farmer.

"Right you are. I'll do that," said Jack.

And he made no mistakes this time, I can tell you.

Bunches

Penelope Farmer

Identical twin sisters, Henrietta and Harriet, known as Henry and Harry, enjoy confusing their school friends as to which is which. After a trying day at school their teacher thinks of a way to tell them apart. The twins have other ideas.

Next morning at school Miss Jenkins said, "Now, Henry and Harry. Now, everyone. Who can think of some way of telling Henry from Harry, so that we stop getting them all muddled up?"

"They can wear badges with their names on," suggested Thomas.

Henry and Harry looked at each other and shook their heads. They didn't want to be the only ones in the class with name badges on.

"Why can't Harry always wear a blue jumper and Henry a red one?" asked Susie.

Again Henry and Harry shook their heads. They both liked wearing blue jumpers one day and red the next.

"Well, I've an idea," said Miss Jenkins. "They can wear different coloured bands on their bunches. And then we'll always know which twin is which."

When Mum came to fetch them at home time, Henry and Harry

told her all about Miss Jenkins's idea. Mum, too, thought it was a good idea for Henry and Harry to have different coloured bands on their bunches.

"I want red bands on mine," said Henry.

"So do I want red bands on mine," said Harry.

"Well, you can't *both* have red bands," said Mum. "How about you having blue bands, Harry?"

"All right," said Harry.

So it was settled. Everyone in Henry and Harry's class knew that the twin with red bands on her bunches was Henry, that the twin with blue bands on her bunches was Harry. Even Thomas and Susie didn't need their special signals any more to know which twin was their best friend and which twin wasn't.

But one day, Henry said to Harry, "I like being Harry sometimes instead of Henry. I like people muddling us up."

"So do I," said Harry.

"Well, *I've* got a good idea now," said Henry. And she whispered something to Harry.

"That's a very good idea. Let's do it tomorrow," Harry whispered back.

Next day, as usual, Mum fixed red bands to Henry's bunches and blue ones to Harry's. But after the twins had hung up their coats in their class cloakroom, they hid behind the end row of pegs and Henry took the red bands off her bunches and put them on Harry's,

and Harry took the blue bands off her bunches and tied them onto Henry's.

Then they went into their classroom and sat down in their places. Or rather, Harry, wearing the red bands on bunches that weren't nearly so neat as when Mum had tied them, sat down in Henry's place. And Henry, wearing blue bunches on *her* not-so-neat bunches, sat down in Harry's.

Miss Jenkins got up to read the register.

"Henry," she called. And Henry almost answered "Here", forgetting she was supposed to be Harry today. Harry kicked her. "Here," she said. And when Miss Jenkins called "Harry?" this time Henry remembered she was Harry and shouted, "Here" loudly. And both of them giggled.

"What's got into you twins today?" said Miss Jenkins.

Henry whispered to Harry, "This is *fun*."

There was only one problem. Even though Henry and Harry were twins, they didn't do the same things *all* the time.

They had different reading books, for instance. Henry's was about Pinky the Pirate. Harry's was about a girl called Jemima. Henry knew all the hard words in Pinky the Pirate, but she didn't know all the hard words in Harry's book about Jemima.

"I am disappointed in you today, Harry," said Miss Jenkins. "You'll have to read that page to me all over again."

Miss Jenkins didn't say she was disappointed in Harry, though. Harry did get some of the hard words in Henry's book right. And Miss Jenkins said she could go to the projects table and stick some more prickles on Henry's model of Sonic the Hedgehog.

Harry was pleased. But Henry

wasn't. It was her model, really.
She didn't want Harry sticking
prickles on Sonic the Hedgehog.
Her face went red. She pinched
Harry.

"What's the matter with you,
Henry?" said Miss Jenkins.

"I want to work on my model,
too," said Henry.

"But you can't, Henry. I want
you to read to me again," said Miss
Jenkins.

At playtime Henry looked out for
Thomas, as usual. But then she
realized that because she was
Harry today, Thomas wasn't her
best friend, Susie was. And that if
Susie was her best friend, she
wasn't going to be able to play
with Thomas's Action Man.

Susie had brought her Puppy in

my Pocket to school that day. But
Henry didn't feel like playing with
Puppy in my Pocket. She went up
to Thomas and pulled her ear, so
that Thomas would know she was
really Henry, even though she was
wearing Harry's blue bands. But
Thomas only said, "Why are you
making Henry's signal, Harry?"

At dinner time, Henry said,
"Shall we change our bands back,
Harry? Then you can be Harry
again, and I can be Henry."

"Oh no," said Harry. "I'm having
a lovely time. Let's stay being each
other till going home time."

"All right," said Henry, a little
sadly.

They had painting in the
afternoon. Henry did a picture of
Miss Jenkins. She thought it was

...er best paintings. So did
...enkins. She pinned it up on
...wall. She wrote underneath it:
"Harry painted a picture of Miss
Jenkins." But Henry thought,
Harry didn't paint it; Henry did.

At playtime Henry found a big
black feather in the playground
and gave it to Miss Jenkins to put
on the nature table. Miss Jenkins
labelled it: "Harry found a crow's
feather." But Henry thought,
Harry didn't find it. I did.

Harry was sorry that Henry was
upset. She found a big white
pebble and put it on the nature
table. Miss Jenkin wrote
underneath it: "Henry found this
pebble." But Henry didn't want her
name under a big white pebble.
She wanted it under her big black

crow's feather.

At last it was home time. Mum came to meet them with baby James in the pushchair. Henry still had Harry's blue bands on her bunches. Harry still had Henry's red ones. Just the same, Mum knew which of them was Henry and which was Harry.

"How's my Henry?" she asked, giving her a big hug. "And how's my Harry?"

"'Enry," said James, giving Henry a big smile. "'Arry," he said, smiling at Harry.

Henry felt happy. Because even if she was still wearing Harry's blue bands, she felt like Henry again.

When Harry said, "It was fun being you all day, Henry," Henry answered, "But I like being me better, don't you, Harry?"

And then she said to Mum, "It's Christmas soon and I know what *I* want Father Christmas to bring me. I want an Action Man, just like Thomas's."

"And I want him to bring *me* Puppy in my Pocket," said Harry.

When Pig Went to Heaven

James Marshall

When Miss Lola the new
schoolteacher came to
town, Pig fell head-over-heels in
love. Miss Lola was the prettiest,
sweetest-smelling pig he'd ever
met.

"She's the one," said Pig.

And he asked her for a date. Miss
Lola, who was on the shy side, said
no. Pig was heartbroken. But
every day he sent flowers to the
schoolhouse and put his poems in

Miss Lola's mailbox. And Miss Lola agreed to a date.

"Next Saturday night at six thirty?" said Pig.

"Fine," said Miss Lola. "I like to eat early."

Pig was overjoyed.

On Thursday Pig stopped by the barber's to have the coarse hairs on his snout trimmed.

"Saturday night, eh?" said the barber. "Where are you taking her?"

"I'm not sure," said Pig.

"I hear Chez Marcel is the best restaurant in town," said the baker, who'd stopped in for his daily shave.

"Then Chez Marcel it is," said Pig.

"Chez Marcel is very fancy," said

the barber. "You will have to wear a tie. And I hope your table manners are OK."

Now Pig had never been to a first-class restaurant. He always ate at Porker O'Shaunessy's Hamburger Haven down the road. And he was *always* there when the three-for-one special was on.

"Do you know about the little fork and the big fork?" said the barber.

"There are *two* forks?" asked Pig.

"The small fork is for appetizers or salads," said the butcher.

"I love salads," said Pig.

"Pay attention, Pig," said the baker. "And the bigger fork is for your main course."

"I see," said Pig, who was already confused.

"You will impress Miss Lola if you speak in French," said the barber. "Just a few words will do. Say *Bonjour* to Monsieur Marcel when you arrive (it means 'good day'), and when you are seated, ask for *La carte, s'il vous plaît* (which means 'the menu, if you please')."

"I know that," said Pig.

"I have an idea," said the barber. "Let's do a practice run. We'll pretend this is Chez Marcel."

A card table and two chairs were set up in the middle of the barbershop.

"Now go out and come back in," said the barber to Pig.

"What a great idea," said Pig.

He went outside and came back in.

"Hi, guys!" he said.

"*No, no, no!*" said the baker. "You must say *Bonjour, Monsieur Marcel.*"

"*Bonjour, Monsieur Marcel,*" said Pig.

"I think he's got it!" said the barber.

"Now offer Miss Lola the nicest seat," said the baker.

"Miss Lola's not here," said Pig.

"We're *pretending!*" said the barber.

"Oh," said Pig.

All afternoon and most of the next day Pig was instructed in the art of good restaurant manners. With the exception of a few mistakes, Pig seemed to get the hang of it.

"Now comes the hard part," said

the barber. "Making interesting and amusing conversation."

"Huh?" said Pig.

"Ladies prefer gentlemen who can keep them amused," explained the barber. "I'll pretend I'm Miss Lola."

And he sat down across from Pig and batted his eyelashes.

"Now say something amusing."

"Er . . ." said Pig. "Do you like Brussels sprouts?"

"Oh dear," said the barber. "We have more work to do."

For hours and hours Pig practised making interesting and amusing conversation.

"Read any good books lately?" said Pig.

"I've just seen the most beautifully written play," said Pig.

"Would you care to hear one of my poems?" said Pig.

"No," said the barber. "Not that."

At six thirty a taxi pulled up at Miss Lola's house. Miss Lola was ready and waiting and peeking out the window. Pig came to the door, handed Miss Lola a beautiful corsage, escorted her to the taxi, and they were off.

Monsieur Marcel himself greeted them at the door of his restaurant.

"*Bonjour, Monsieur Marcel*," said Pig.

Miss Lola was impressed.

And Monsieur Marcel gave them the best table in the house.

Pig put his napkin in his lap.

"*La carte, si'il vous plaît*," he said to the waiter. "That means 'the menu, if you please'."

"I know," said the waiter.

"Oh Pig," said Miss Lola. "What a lovely place."

"Glad you like it," said Pig. "I come here quite often."

Miss Lola and Pig studied the menu.

"I'll start off with a crisp green salad," said Miss Lola. "And then

I'll have the chef's special."

"Me too," said Pig.

That was easy, he thought.

While dinner was being prepared, Pig tried to make interesting and amusing conversation. At first it was slow going.

"Read any good books lately?"

"Not really," said Miss Lola.

"I just saw the most beautifully written play," said Pig.

"What was it called?" asked Miss Lola.

"I forgot," said Pig.

"Do you have any more of your poems?" said Miss Lola.

Pig was delighted. And until dinner was served, he recited his poetry.

"Ooh," said Miss Lola.

The waiter brought the salads.

"*Merci*," said Pig.

He was delighted that things were going so well.

Then Pig noticed that Miss Lola had stuck her snout directly into her salad and was noisily munching away. There was a lot of slurping, grunting, and intake of air. Pig picked up his fork.

"I never use forks," said Miss Lola. "They're so silly."

"I agree," said Pig, who'd become adept at using a fork and wanted to show off.

Then Miss Lola dropped some of her lettuce on the floor, picked it up with a swoop, and popped it into her mouth. Other diners couldn't help but notice, and whispered among themselves.

"I'm thirsty," said Miss Lola.
Pig ordered a bottle of mineral
water.

"Not the bubbly kind," he said.
When the mineral water was
brought, Miss Lola said, "I'll do
that." And she bit off the plastic
cap.

Later Miss Lola ordered three
desserts and devoured them in no

261

time flat. She had gobs of whipped cream all over her snout and some in her ears.

"I liked the eclairs best," she said.

"Have another one," said Pig, who'd brought a lot of money and wasn't worried about the bill.

Miss Lola picked her teeth and burped so loudly that all conversation in the restaurant came to a halt.

At the door of the restaurant Monsieur Marcel said goodbye to them personally.

"Do come again, please," he said. "It's so gratifying to have customers who really know how to enjoy their food."

On the way home Pig asked the driver to pull over and stop.

Then he and Miss Lola got out and had a lovely mudbath in a ditch by the side of the road.

"You really know how to entertain a girl," said Miss Lola.

And Pig was in heaven.

ACKNOWLEDGEMENTS

The publishers wish to thank the following for permission to reproduce copyright material:

Tony Bradman: "Dilly and the Horror Film" from *Dilly Goes to School* by Tony Bradman; first published by Methuen Children's Books 1987 and reproduced by permission of Egmont Children's Books Ltd.

Pamela Oldfield: "Melanie Brown is Too Helpful" from *Melanie Brown Climbs a Tree* by Pamela Oldfield; first published by Faber & Faber Ltd 1972 and reproduced with their permission.

Magdalen Nabb: "Josie Smith and the Concert" from *Josie Smith at School* by Magdalen Nabb; first published by Collins Children's Books 1990 and reproduced by permission of HarperCollins Publishers.

Margaret Mahy: "Trouble in the Supermarket" from *Nonstop Nonsense* by Margaret Mahy; first published by J.M. Dent & Sons and reproduced by permission of Orion Children's Books.

Margaret Mahy: "Patrick Comes to School" from *The Second Margaret Mahy Story Book* by Margaret Mahy; first published by J.M. Dent & Sons and reproduced by permission of Orion Children's Books.

Francesca Simon: "Perfect Peter's Horrid Day" from *Horrid Henry and the Secret Club* by Francesca Simon; first published by Orion Children's Books 1995 and reproduced with their permission.

Andrew Matthews: "Lazy Jack" from *Silly Stories* by Andrew Matthews: first published by Orion Children's Books 1994 and reproduced with their permission.

Ann Cameron: "Chef Huey" from *The Stories Huey Tells* by Ann Cameron; first published by Victor Gollancz/Hamish Hamilton 1995 and © Ann Cameron 1995; reproduced by permission of Penguin Books Ltd.

David Henry Wilson: "Getting Rich with Jeremy James" by David Henry Wilson; first published by Chatto & Windus 1979 and reproduced by permission of Random House UK Ltd.

Kaye Umansky: "King Keith and the Nasty Case of Dragonitus" from *King Keith and the Nasty Case of Dragonitus and Cousin Clive* by Kaye Umansky;

ACKNOWLEDGEMENTS

first published by Penguin 1990 and reproduced by permission of the Caroline Sheldon Literary Agency on behalf of the author.

George Summerfield: "Vardiello" from *Tale Two* by Geoffrey Summerfield; first published by Ward Lock Educational and reproduced by permission of Clare Summerfield on behalf of the Estate of the author.

Penelope Farmer; "Bunches" from *Twin Trouble* by Penelope Farmer; Text © Penelope Farmer 1992; reproduced by permission of the publisher Walker Books Ltd., London.

Philippa Werry; "The Day Michael Made the News"; first published in "School Journal" 1:3, 1993 and reproduced by permission of Philippa Werry and Learning Media, New Zealand.

James Marshall; "When Pig Went to Heaven" from *Rats on the Range and Other Stories* by James Marshall; copyright © 1993 by the Estate of James Marshall.

Every effort has been made to trace the copyright holders but where this has not been possible or where any error has been made the publishers will be pleased to make the necessary arrangement at the first opportunity.